Tales

By Charles Todd

The Ian Rutledge Mysteries

The Bess Crawford Mysteries

Other Fiction

Tales

Short Stories Featuring
Ian Rutledge and Bess Crawford

CHARLES TODD

WITNESS
IMPULSE

An Imprint of HarperCollinsPublishers

EPub Edition July 2015 ISBN: 9780062443755

Print Edition ISBN: 9780062443762
HB 07.22.2021

Contents

Contents

Introduction

HERE IN THIS mini-anthology are two Inspector Ian Rutledge and two Bess Crawford tales for you to savor while waiting for the next pub date for the mystery novels! We love writing short stories, and many of them are about one or the other of our favorite characters. It's an exciting way for us to get to know them even better. This collection is for you, after many requests for a print as well as an e-book edition. Enjoy!

Caroline and Charles

THE KIDNAPPING

*An Ian Rutledge Original
Short Story*

London 1920

IT WAS LATE, the rain coming down hard, when the man hurried through the main door of Scotland Yard and came to an abrupt halt as he saw the sergeant at the desk.

"I must speak to an inspector at once," he said, his voice that of a gentleman though his clothes were torn and disheveled, his hat wet and filthy.

"If you'll give me your name, sir," the sergeant said calmly, reaching for a sheet of paper, "and the particulars."

"I tell you, I need an inspector. Look at me, man! Do I look as if I have all night to answer your questions?"

"All the same, sir—"

"Damn it," the man said, and turned toward the door to one side of the desk.

"Here!" the sergeant exclaimed, rising. "You can't go in there until you've told me your business."

But the man was too quick for him and had reached the door just as it opened.

The tall, dark-haired man standing there looked from the agitated sergeant to the flushed and angry stranger.

"Inspector Rutledge, sir? This man refuses to give his name and his reasons for coming to the Yard.

"Inspector?" the intruder exclaimed, stepping back. "Thank God. I've just been robbed and beaten, and my daughter has been taken away by force. You must help me find her. Cecily is only twelve, she'll be terrified by now. I can't bear to think what she's suffering."

"Where was this?" Rutledge asked.

"On Christopher Street. Number 10. We'd just returned home from dinner with friends—this was a little after ten o'clock—and as we stepped out of the cab, two men accosted us. Before I quite knew what was happening, they had knocked me to the ground, kicking me repeatedly while a third man, our erstwhile cabbie, had caught my daughter by the arms and forced her back into the waiting cab. I was only half conscious when the two attacking me went through my pockets but took nothing, not my watch, not even my purse. I couldn't stop them, couldn't even cry out. And then they leapt into the cab and it set off at a fast pace, disappearing around the next corner before I managed to get to my feet and attempted to go after them."

Rutledge regarded him. "Your face isn't damaged."

"No, they kicked me, I tell you. My ribs, my back, my shoulders."

"Have you seen a doctor? Mr.—"

"Dunstan. Charles Dunstan. In God's name, how can I think about going to a doctor when Cecily is in the hands of those brutes? She's in danger, I tell you, and you must help me find her. What do they want with her? I'm not a wealthy man, I can't pay a great ransom for her. That's what frightens me. She's a pretty child." He fumbled for his wallet and brought out a photograph of a young girl with long fair hair and a sweet smile.

Rutledge studied it and returned the photograph. "Why didn't you find a constable, set the police after them straightaway, rather than take the time coming here?"

"There was no constable in sight. Should I have lost time finding him? This is a Yard matter, surely, not the London police. I beg of you, *do* something."

"Did you see the faces of these three men? Or of the cabbie?"

"No. He was just the cabbie, I paid him no heed until he leapt down to take my daughter. By that time, the other two had come out of the shadows before I could even turn and defend myself."

"Did they speak?"

"No. The attack seemed all the worse for being carried out in complete silence."

"Why had you taken a cab in the first place?"

"We'd had dinner with Mr. and Mrs. Lowery."

"Old friends?"

"I've known them a year or two. He's a member of my club."

He put a hand to his ribs as he coughed, and Rutledge said, "Here, sit down." Over Dunstan's shoulder, Rutledge said to the Sergeant, "Send men to Number 10 Christopher Street, and three more to find this cabbie—or if possible, what became of the cab after the crime."

The sergeant said, "There's only the night staff on duty."

"Then summon more men. I'll take Mr. Dunstan to my office."

He led the way up the stairs and along the passage to an office overlooking the street.

Mr. Dunstan, inspecting it, saying, "You *are* an inspector, are you not?"

Rutledge smiled. "Not precisely the accommodations of a banker, but I am most assuredly an inspector."

"Perhaps I should speak to someone of greater seniority."

"You'll be hard-pressed to find anyone of greater seniority at this hour of a Saturday night. For my sins, I'm on duty until the morning."

Dunstan sat down, wincing as he reached to set his hat on the table against the wall. "Very well, tell me what we are to do about recovering my daughter."

"First we must see what can be discovered at the scene, and where the cabbie may have got to. I'll be leaving shortly for Christopher Street myself. But first I must ask if you have any enemies. And where, if you are here alone, is the child's mother?"

"She's dead. These past three years. As for enemies—I can't think of any who would have taken out their animosity on my child."

"Then you do have enemies?" Rutledge said.

"I am a King's Counsel, Inspector. I have tried many men who have threatened to make me regret my part in sending them to prison."

"And personal enemies, rather than professional?"

"My late wife's brother. His name is Roland Paley. But he's in western Canada. Vancouver. Has been for some twenty years. We quarreled when I married Grace. That was fifteen years ago. The family's choice was a wealthy man in the City, much older than Grace. I was a struggling barrister then, not likely to provide for her as he could. Ours was a love match, you see. Her father finally came round, but her mother and her brother felt that she was merely infatuated with me, and in time would come to regret the match."

"And did she?"

"Never."

Rutledge rose. "I'll ask you to remain here, if you will. I have work to do, but it's important to know where to find you."

"I can't sit here!"

"You have come to the police, Mr. Dunstan. Let them do their work."

"I'll run mad with worry! At the very least, let me come with you."

And so they found themselves out in the rain, taking Rutledge's motorcar to Christopher Street.

There were two constables and a sergeant already there, combing the scene with their torches, their capes slick with rain.

Rutledge said, pulling his hat lower to shield his eyes, "Anything?"

Sergeant Dickens shook his head. "Not even a drop of blood."

"And the neighbors?"

"Constable Hudson is speaking to them now, sir. So far, it appears they were all cozy in front of the fire with the drapes drawn. Not one heard anything, nor saw anything."

Rutledge turned to Dunstan. "Did your daughter cry out?"

"The man holding her must have had a hand over her mouth. I didn't hear her cry. He turned her away from the beating I was taking, then shoved her in the cab."

"And she didn't struggle?"

"I was frantically defending myself. I only know that I didn't hear her scream."

Which was, Rutledge thought, decidedly odd. If a girl of twelve was being torn from her father's side by strangers on a dark, rainy night, she would not have gone quietly with her captors.

A constable came walking briskly toward them. Sergeant Dickens looked up and said, "What is it?"

"The Yard sent me to tell you, sir, that the cab has been found. It was left in a street in Chelsea."

"And what if anything was in it?" the sergeant demanded.

"No one, sir. And nothing inside that would indicate why it was being abandoned as it was. The horse was standing there waiting. No drops or smears of blood. But there was one interesting thing, sir." He held out his hand. In his palm lay a coin, dark and hardly visible.

Rutledge picked it up. "A penny. A Canadian penny."

"Yes, sir. There's no way to know who dropped it, or when. But it was there, and I made note of it."

"Thank you, Constable. Take two men and see if you can locate the missing cabbie. Was he one of the kidnappers—or is he lying injured or dead somewhere? Look in the hospitals as well. He may have been found and taken there before we knew of the kidnapping."

The constable touched his helmet and was gone, trotting back the way he'd come, his boots loud in the quiet night on such a quiet street.

"A Canadian penny," Dunstan said, holding out his hand for it. Rutledge gave it to him, and he added, "There's no way to tell the date. It's rather worn." He turned it this way and that in the torchlight.

"Did you keep in touch with your brother-in-law?" Rutledge asked. "Would he have reason to know where you lived?"

"We were living in Number 10 at the time of my wife's death. I cabled him, but he never replied."

"Why would he wish to harm your daughter?"

"I can't think why he would," Dunstan said. "Yes, he could very likely still harbor a grudge against me. But Cecily? No. He's never even met her."

"Did your attackers have good reason to believe they might have killed you, after the beating here, outside your door?" Rutledge looked up and down the street, but there was no sign of a scuffle, and only Dunstan's word that the kidnapping had even occurred. Except for the very real fear in the man's eyes.

Dunstan looked up at Rutledge's face, shadowed by the brim of his hat. "Do you know, they could well have. I lay there, having troubles breathing from the blows. I'd fought back at first, but I couldn't go on. It was all I could do to drag myself to my feet as they leapt into the cab and drove off."

"We'll cable the Vancouver police. If your brother-in-law is still there, we'll have to strike him from our list of suspects." He summoned one of his men and gave the instructions.

"He could have sent others to do his work for him. But why? I can't think of a reason. I've told you, I'm not a wealthy man. Comfortable, yes. But hardly able to pay a ransom that would make such an enterprise worth anyone's while."

"It may not be a matter of ransom," Rutledge pointed out.

"Yes, well, what other use could he possibly have for taking his sister's child?"

Their search of Christopher Street had yielded no new information. Rutledge said to Dunstan, "I'd like to have a look in your house."

"But I was attacked out here."

"Nevertheless."

"It's a waste of time, but yes, come inside."

He went up the steps of Number 10, and unlocked the door. "I'm grateful they left my keys," he said as the door swung open.

Rutledge found himself in a short entry and through the next door saw that he was facing a staircase with more doors to either side of it.

When he opened the right hand door, Dunstan said, "The drawing room—"

He stopped, appalled at the sight before them.

The room had been ransacked. And not gently.

"My God," he murmured, standing there in the doorway.

"Don't touch anything," Rutledge warned. "Show me the other rooms."

They found that the study had also been ransacked as well as the master bedroom. But the rest of the house appeared not to have been touched save for a broken window in the kitchen.

"What the hell were they after?" Dunstan demanded. "I don't keep any papers here. Or much in the way of valuables. My late wife's jewelry, which will go to Cecily when she's older. My will. My accounts."

"But they must have believed something was here to find. Do you have any live-in staff? If you do, then we must get to them at once."

"No, not since Cecily outgrew her governess. She goes to a day school now. The cook, the housekeeper, and the maids leave at seven every evening."

"When did you go out to dine tonight?" Rutledge asked, surveying the damage done to a lovely maple chest at the foot of the bed.

"A little after seven. Mr. and Mrs. Lowery had been wanting to meet Cecily. Their nephew is coming to stay while his parents travel, and they're anxious to find a good school."

"Did your daughter enjoy her evening?"

"Oh, yes, very much so. She's—she's looking forward to meeting Stephen."

"She wasn't uncomfortable amongst the adults?"

"Not at all. They made much of her."

"It's likely that someone came here to search the house, knowing you were not at home. And not finding what they were after, arranged to meet you when you left the Lowery house. Who knew you were dining out? After dinner, did you have trouble summoning a cab?"

"I expect Cecily told any number of her friends. And the staff knew we weren't dining in. My clerks because I was leaving chambers early. As for finding a cab when the evening was over, one was coming up Jermaine Street at that moment. I got the impression he'd just set down a passenger. I thought myself lucky." Dunstan grimaced.

Rutledge turned and went to the door. "My motorcar is just outside. I think we'd better have a look at the situation at the Lowery house."

Dunstan followed him, pausing only to lock the door, saying as he did so, "I don't remember anyone on the street when the cabbie stopped here."

Rutledge pointed to the servants' stairs half hidden by shrubbery along the railing. "As good a hiding place as any."

They found Jermaine Street quiet when they arrived. Like Christopher Street, it was upper middle class, the houses large and comfortable, the neighborhood respectable. Hardly the scene of any crime. Rutledge left his motorcar several doors away from Number 16, and they went the rest of the way on foot. Rutledge carried his torch in his hand. There were lights on in the house, mostly on the floors above, as the family prepared for bed. Rutledge continued past Number 16 to the corner, searching the stair wells leading to the servants' entrance and even the small square with its gated garden and ornamental trees. On the far side of the square, at Number 23, he discovered the cabbie lying in a pool of blood at the foot of the servant stairs.

Rutledge felt for a pulse. "He's alive. A blow on the head, as far as I can tell," he said, shining his torch on the dark matting in the man's graying hair. "Knock on the door. We'll need an ambulance."

Dunstan did as he was told, rousing the household and asking for the use of their telephone. When the cabbie had been taken away and the anxious owner of Number 23 had been reassured that he wouldn't be murdered in his bed that night, Rutledge also put in a telephone call to the Yard, asking for men to examine the street. Meanwhile the local constable had come past on his rounds and could say with certainty that there was no body in the servants' entrance when he looked at half past nine.

"The kidnappers must have taken a cab to this address, overcome the driver, and prepared to meet you when you came out of the Lowery house, assuming that you wouldn't be too late in leaving given your daughter was with you."

"I'm relieved that they didn't kill the poor man. Or me. At least that gives me hope I shall find my daughter alive."

"The question is," Rutledge said, "how did they know you weren't at home in Christopher Street when they came to search the house? And how did they know to look for you at Jermaine Street when they didn't find whatever it is they wanted? We must interview your servants." He beckoned to a young constable. "Give him the names and directions for your staff, if you please."

"I can't believe they would betray me in this fashion. They've been with me these twelve years!"

"They can be bribed. Or cajoled into talking to a caller at the door. Or they can be a party to what happened."

Dunstan gave the names to the constable, and Rutledge sent him off to interview the women.

The rain was heavy again, the gutters running with rainwater, and in spite of his umbrella, his shoulders were nearly wet through as he looked across the square at the now-dark Lowery residence.

"What could they want?" Dunstan asked, pacing restlessly. "I have tried to think of anything, anything at all, that would be worth taking Cecily in this way."

"Revenge. Money. Fear. There can be a long list of reasons. Did your wife live in Canada?"

"For a time, yes. Her father was sent out there by his firm. He was a mining engineer. He told me once that if he'd been clever, he might have discovered for himself the gold that later started the famous Gold Rush in the Yukon. Instead, he was looking for other minerals."

"Did he own property in Canada?"

"A shooting camp in the woods. He sometimes went there with friends. My wife inherited it, but neither of us has ever been there. Her brother often uses it without asking, but I never pursued the matter. It was the principle that irritated me, that he felt he should have inherited it and behaved as if it were indeed his."

"Why your wife, if it was a shooting camp?" Rutledge asked as they crossed the square.

"I expect it was because her father never really liked Elston. He was a troublesome child and grew into a troublesome man."

They had reached the Lowery house. Rutledge knocked, but it was several minutes before the door opened. A thin, balding man stood there in his dressing gown. His brows rose in surprise.

"I say, Dunstan." His glance moved on to Rutledge.

"Andrew, Cecily has been kidnapped," Dunstan said before Rutledge could speak. "We're trying to find her."

"May we come in?" Rutledge asked.

Lowery stepped to one side. "Yes, of course. Are you serious, Dunstan? Cecily? What in God's name has happened?" He led them into the drawing room and lit the lamp. "I don't understand."

"How many people knew you'd invited Mr. Dunstan and his daughter to dinner?"

"How many people? Good God, I have no idea. I never made a secret of it." He looked up as his wife came into room. "My dear, it's distressing news—something has happened to Cecily."

"But she was just here," she exclaimed. "I don't understand." She was a fair woman, attractive and slim.

Dunstan told her what had happened. "And we've just found the cabbie, across the square. He's on his way to hospital. The police haven't been able to question him."

Mrs. Lowery's gaze moved to Rutledge's face. "But the Yard is doing everything that's possible, surely!"

"Can you give me a list of the other guests this evening?" he asked. "And tell me whether they left before or after Dunstan and his daughter?"

"But of course." She went to the small desk by the door and sat down to write.

Rutledge said, "The Dunstan house was ransacked. Whoever took Cecily Dunstan didn't find what he was looking for there, nor on Mr. Dunstan's person. That could well explain why his daughter was taken."

"Holding her—but that's diabolic!" Mrs. Lowery said. "Is it money?"

"There have been no demands for ransom," Dunstan said, the beginnings of panic in his voice.

"Early days," Rutledge pointed out. "They'll wait until you are ready to do anything to retrieve your daughter."

"They needn't wait. I've already reached that point," Dunstan answered.

Mrs. Lowery finished the list and passed it to Rutledge.

There were two other couples and a single woman, Dunstan making up the numbers. Mr. and Mrs. Carson, Mr. and Mrs. Frey, and Miss Abernathy. Two men and three women. There had been three men in the attack on the Dunstans. If Carson and Frey were involved, then Lowery himself would have had to be a party to the kidnapping of Cecily Dunstan. Was Dunstan mistaken or had he lied about his attackers? Or were those three men unconnected with the dinner party?

"The Carsons are old friends," Mrs. Lowery was adding. "We met the Freys six months ago. They'd been in Kenya for some years and have just returned to England. Miss Abernathy is traveling with them, at the request of her parents."

"Thank you." Rutledge studied the short list. "Why were they in Kenya?" he asked.

"Something was said about growing coffee," Lowery replied. "Miss Abernathy told us her father is the doctor in Nairobi."

Mrs. Lowery smiled. "She's quite charming, kept all of us laughing with tales of her life out there. Her story about trying to stalk and shoot a springbok in Ngorongoro Crater had us all laughing."

"Indeed?"

"I can't believe that our guests—it's not likely that they're involved with this," Lowery said. "To what end?"

"It's what they may have seen as they left your house that interests me."

"Yes, of course."

Rutledge asked for their direction and was sent to a hotel near Kensington Palace.

Dunstan said, "I'm sorry to pull them out of bed," as he and Rutledge took the narrow elevator to the third floor. "But for Cecily's sake, we have no choice."

Miss Abernathy was in Number 307 and Rutledge knocked at her door first.

A sleepy voice called, "Who is it?"

"The police, Miss Abernathy. There's been a thief in the hotel. I need to make certain that you're all right."

"Yes. Yes, I am."

"Could you come to the door and verify you are not being held against your will?"

Dunstan said, "What the hell—" but Rutledge silenced him with a raised hand.

"I'm in bed," the voice behind the door said plaintively. "Must I?"

"I'm afraid so," Rutledge answered.

There was a long silence, and then Miss Abernathy came to the door, her long red hair spilling down the back of her dressing gown.

"As you can see, I'm perfectly fine," she told him. "Now am I allowed to return to my—" At that moment she recognized Dunstan, over her shoulder.

With an angry cry, she shouted, "Tom!" and made to slam the door in Rutledge's face. But she hadn't reckoned with his quick reflexes.

Rutledge's shoe was in the crack, and his shoulder hit the door in the same instant, propelling her back into the room where she stumbled and fell against the bed. She was still calling for Tom, and Rutledge wheeled as Dunstan shouted, meeting the man as he charged into the room.

"Police," Rutledge warned him, but he didn't stop. They grappled, Tom driven by fury. Rutledge was slowly getting the better of him when the woman from the bed threw herself on his back, and another woman ran into the room, her hands out like claws, attacking Dunstan. He swore as her nails raked his face, then beat her fists against his chest.

There was a faint sound from the wardrobe behind him. Dunstan, hearing it, caught the woman by the shoulders, spinning her around with some force, and whipped the dangling sash of her dressing gown around her wrists before shoving her into a chair. Then he went at the door like a madman, flinging it open and saying something Rutledge couldn't catch.

Rutledge was able to put his shoulder into the next blow, and the man fell to the floor, dazed. He turned on Miss Abernathy and, without ceremony, snapped his handcuffs over her wrists and pushed her back down on the bed. He wheeled to where Dunstan was standing in front of the wardrobe, trying to lift his daughter out of the cramped space but his ribs wouldn't allow him to shift her. She had been bound with cloths, and there was barely room for her to crouch. Rutledge stepped forward, lifted her out of the wardrobe and carried her to the only other chair in the room. Dunstan began to tear at the knots but Rutledge brought out a pocket knife and quickly cut them.

The odor of ether was on her clothing, and in a black rage, her father turned on the man Miss Abernathy had called Tom. "You dined with us, you bastard, and when we left, you attacked us and used ether on my child."

Frey scrambled away from Dunstan's fury, putting the bed between them, but that didn't stop the outraged father. He launched himself across the bed, shoving Miss Abernathy out of his way, and caught the man by the throat. It was all Rutledge could do to pull him off Frey, as Dunstan's hands tightened their grip.

"Go downstairs," he told the struggling, angry father. "Find a policeman and bring him here, then take my motorcar and drive to the Yard. We need help and we need it straightaway."

"I'm not leaving my daughter," Dunstan said stubbornly.

"She's just regaining consciousness. Do as I say and bring a doctor back with you. She should be seen."

Dunstan turned to look at his daughter, her eyes closed, her mouth slack, and her face very pale.

"Dear God," he said, and was out the door, leaving it wide. Rutledge could hear his footsteps racing down the carpeted corridor.

Rutledge turned to the three people eyeing him speculatively. "If you try something," he said tightly, "it will give me great pleasure to use you as Dunstan would have done. In the name," he added, "of quelling an attempted escape."

Frey said, "We outnumber you three to one. Even with their hands tied." He nodded toward his two companions.

Rutledge smiled coldly. And waited. He watched the two women and one man weigh their chances against the tall, broad-shouldered young policeman, and then subside. Cowards, he found himself thinking, who would leap out at a man and kidnap his daughter but who were unwilling to try their luck with someone who was their match.

After a moment Miss Abernathy said, "We covered our tracks well. How did you know?"

He crossed to the door and swung it closed. "The fact that there were three assailants, and you were three to dine. That you left shortly before the Dunstans, with time to set up your trap. Three people dressed as men, to confuse the police. It was a well-prepared plan, and working it through the unsuspecting Lowerys was clever. But I was certain when I told Miss Abernathy here that a thief was on the loose in the hotel and she showed no concern. A woman alone in a strange city would have been frightened enough to welcome the assurance of a policeman making certain she was safe. But she couldn't afford to have the police come into her room."

"That's ridiculous," Miss Abernathy exclaimed. "I was glad you'd come to my door."

But she hadn't been.

That was all he could pry out of them. He went to sit beside Cecily, assuring her that she was safe as she sat up and stared with frightened eyes at her abductors. Finally Dunstan arrived with two men from the Yard and a doctor. As the constables took charge of the surly kidnappers, the doctor was bending over Cecily, examining her while reassuring her that all was well.

A few minutes later, the doctor crossed the room to speak Rutledge. "She'll be all right," he said, "but ether is measured by drops according to weight, not just poured onto a handkerchief. They took a serious risk."

Dunstan said wearily, still kneeling by his daughter, "Whatever those people wanted, it must be valuable indeed."

"We'll find out in due course," Rutledge replied. "First we need to establish just who they really are, and where they came from. That could also tell us what they were after. They'll be in prison, meanwhile. You and your daughter will have nothing more to fear from them."

He could tell that Dunstan was dubious. The night's events had shaken him badly.

It wasn't until a cable to Canada was answered that they had what they needed.

Roland Paley dead of heart attack ten months ago. Widow remarried to one Thomas Cochran Frey. Whereabouts unknown.

Rutledge brought the news to Dunstan, who said, "But that doesn't explain anything, does it? Unless they took Roland seriously, that he'd been cheated over that blasted hunting lodge."

"I sent a second cable to the Canadian Mounted," he said. "It seems the hunting lodge that your father-in-law left to your wife is quite valuable now. The railroad wants to build a hotel on the property. They're willing to pay huge sums for the lodge and the land. If you could be persuaded to make the deed over in Mrs. Frey's name, she and her husband stood to make a fortune. The police are now looking at the post mortem results for your brother-in-law, to see if he died of natural causes."

"But I would have given them the deed, I knew nothing about Canadian railways," Dunstan said as he and Rutledge sat down in his drawing room. Set to rights again, it was quite handsome. "They didn't need to kidnap my daughter!"

"Greedy people," Rutledge answered, "as a rule judge others by themselves. They wouldn't have handed over a valuable property without a fight. Your daughter was insurance."

"I don't want anything to do with that property now," Dunstan said. "Let them have it if they'll stay away from me and my daughter. It has caused nothing but trouble since my father-in-law's death."

"One isn't allowed to make a profit from a crime. Sell it to the Canadian Pacific Railway yourself and invest the money for your daughter. It will ensure her future if anything should happen to you. And I'm sure that's what your wife would have wished."

"Yes, I'll think about it."

Rutledge left him then, and went back at the Yard.

Sergeant Gibson said as Rutledge came up the stairs, "It could have ended far worse. Kidnappings often do. You were lucky."

Rutledge thanked him and walked on to his office.

Chief Superintendent Bowles came in five minutes later. "You took a terrible risk. You should have sent for a more seasoned officer."

Rutledge smiled. There was no possible way of satisfying his superior. But he said only, "Sergeant Gibson feels it was a matter of luck."

"Yes, well, don't count on luck the next time. Send for assistance." He left, and Rutledge sat down behind his desk.

He hadn't told Dunstan the whole truth. Or Bowles. For it had been good police work that had brought the case to a satisfactory conclusion.

What had triggered his suspicion of Miss Abernathy—who had turned out to be Mrs. Frey's sister, one Josephine Tanner—was a remark made by Mrs. Lowery, that Miss Abernathy had boasted of shooting springbok in Ngorongoro Crater while growing up in Kenya before the war. But the crater was actually in what was then German Tanganyika, not Kenya. And Springbok was native to South Africa, not East Africa. Miss Tanner had enjoyed being the charming Miss Abernathy, amusing the dinner guests, but she'd got her facts wrong.

Pride had been her downfall.

And Rutledge had a geography tutor at Oxford to thank for teaching him about Africa. His name was Pieter Roos and he would have enjoyed learning that his pupil had solved a crime with that knowledge. But he had died in Egypt during the war, and Rutledge hadn't felt like explaining that to Bowles.

THE GIRL ON THE BEACH

A Bess Crawford Mystery

WHEN I SAW her on the strand, like a mermaid who had wandered too near our world, I knew at once that she was dead. The easy, relaxed sleeper enjoying the sun and a warm breeze was very different from a stiff, angular corpse. She had been dead some time, in fact, I realized as I got within a few feet of her. Rigor mortis had set in but not faded yet.

A pretty girl, long dark hair spread under her head and across the white shirtwaist she wore, slim and nicely dressed—but not for an afternoon by the sea. Dark blue walking skirt, good black leather shoes.

I disliked leaving her there, but I had the beach to myself. It was very early and there was no one I could ask to stand watch.

Glancing at the tide, I saw that she was safe from the sea for now. I didn't think it had washed her up, but it could take her away. And on the far side of her, someone had come this far, turned, and walked back. The prints weren't deep enough for him—it was a man's shoe and size—to have carried her and left her here. But he'd found her, as I had, and hurried away.

"I'll come back," I whispered, and turned to run the way I'd walked this morning.

Finding a constable proved harder than I expected, and then I had to explain who I was—a nurse, on leave from *Britannic*—who had driven here for a little peace and quiet. One could still hear the guns in Eastbury, on the Sussex coast, and there was very little beach for me to walk, given the barricades against invasion, but there was no time to go home to Somerset and none of my flatmates were in London just now to cheer me up. Still, it offered solitude.

We walked back together, past the church whispered to be a nest of smugglers two hundred years ago, but serene now in its wooded churchyard.

She was where I'd left her. But someone had been there in my absence. There was a third set of footprints now. And they belonged to a woman.

I pointed these out to Constable Whitaker, and he nodded.

Across the road behind us came more men, including someone I thought must be an inspector. We waited for him, and he knelt to look at the girl. He was graying, too old for the battlefield, staying on at his post like so many people striving to replace the soldiers gone off to war. But his eyes, a keen blue, were young.

"How did you know she was dead?" he asked, not looking up at me.

"I'm a nurse," I said tartly. "We are supposed to recognize the difference between life and death." He hadn't introduced himself, and I wasn't a foolish hysterical girl.

"Do you know what killed her?"

"I didn't touch the body," I said.

"Then let's turn her over, shall we?"

I helped him lift her and we both saw the wound in her back.

"Knifed from behind," he said. "But not here."

There wasn't enough blood for that. "Then where? And whose footprints are those? The second set wasn't here when I discovered her."

The inspector sent a pair of constables to follow the footsteps, then said to me, "We haven't had many murders this spring." He began to search the woman's pockets, but there was nothing to identify her.

It was 1916, the war to end all wars was now two years old, and Britain was getting tired. Working flat out, trying to keep the troops supplied, struggling to bring in what we desperately needed on ships plundered by the German fleet and subs, we had all done our bit as the King had asked, but the human body wasn't a machine, it needed rest and good food and peace. Who still had the energy for anger, much less murder?

I must have said that last aloud, because the inspector looked at me, a hard stare, and said, "Why do you think it was anger—or murder?"

"She couldn't have stabbed herself. The elbow doesn't bend that far. And she wasn't in a struggle with her killer, there are no signs of cuts or scrapes or bruises that I can see. She must have turned away from him. Or her. A lover's quarrel? Or a matter of jealousy?"

She *was* very pretty. He could see that himself.

The inspector got to his feet and introduced himself finally. His name was Robbins. "Bess Crawford," I told him.

"Have you dealt with murder before?"

Not in England. But I'd seen it in India as a child, when we were living there. "No," I answered, rather than explain. "But I deal with dying men and sometimes dying women. It won't help to cry over her. I'd rather see her killer found."

"Very commendable," he said dryly. "Do you ever cry?"

I looked at him. "Often. But I don't think that's your business to ask."

"I'm sorry. That was uncalled for."

One of the constables came trotting back. "The earlier prints lead to the road. I couldn't follow them there. But I did walk through the churchyard. There's a bloody patch by one of the gravestones to the east of the church."

"Good work." Robbins dusted the sand from his fingers.

The doctor was just coming toward us, breathing hard as he made his way over the sandy beach. I could hear him click his tongue when he saw the girl. I understood when he said, "What a pity."

While he finished what he had to do, we stood and stared out to sea, Robbins and I. I could tell he was thinking. And so I stayed quiet.

The other constable called to us. "I think I've found something, sir."

In the palm of his hand he had a small object that I quickly realized was a woman's earring. "It was in the sand. It could belong to anyone but…"

His voice trailed off. I looked at it with interest. An old fashioned piece. Gold, with a citrine in the bob. The part that hooked into the ear had been sprung, and it must have simply slipped out. I reached out to touch the girl's hair. But there were gold studs in her ears, and both were there.

Robbins examined the object. "Find the match and we'll know whether it's important or not," he said, deflating the hopes of the sharp-eyed, elderly constable.

"All right," the doctor said, and Robbins signaled for a stretcher to be brought up. I stayed while they lifted her gently onto the canvas, and I saw in the sand under her body a small scrap of newspaper. Robbins had seen it too, picking it up and smoothing it out in his palm. There was part of an obituary on one side and on the other an advertisement for a companion.

"A clue?" he asked, "or was it here before she put on the beach?"

I had no answer there and he smiled.

I said, "A nurse is trained to observe."

"So is a policeman, Miss Crawford," he told me dryly. "And I don't believe this will help us very much. Unless of course you're looking to apply for a position as companion?"

"Matron would have a few words to say about that," I informed him.

The stretcher was being taken away now, and I turned to follow it. Inspector Robbins spent a few minutes more looking around in the sand, and then caught me up just as we reached the road, where the ambulance was waiting. I watched the girl being put into it, a sheet over her face, and thought again how young she was—my age, perhaps, or a little younger. What had brought her to this place and her death? She was well enough dressed, and she didn't appear to be starving.

As if he'd read my thoughts, Inspector Robbins said, "Someone will look for her. She's not the sort to go missing. There's a family somewhere."

"It will depend on how far she's come to take up that position as companion," I said. "May I see that scrap of newspaper again?"

He reluctantly passed it to me, and I studied both sides.

"This obituary. It's for a soldier. A Captain MacRae. You can trace him through the War Office, I should think. It would tell us what newspaper this came from."

"Would you like to do my work for me, Miss Crawford?"

"No." The ambulance was pulling away. "But I have a feeling she died because she was lured somewhere on purpose."

"And you can infer this from a bit of newspaper?" He smiled. "Come now!"

I looked at him. "I'm sorry, Inspector. Not from the newspaper. I have parents, you see. They wouldn't allow me go wandering about England on a whim. So hers must have thought there was a proper reason for that poor girl to leave home."

"And what if this bit of paper was blowing down the strand early this morning, and her killer never noticed it when he put her down?"

"What if she held on to it as she died, and it slipped through her fingers as she was placed there?"

We went to the churchyard to look at the blood the constable had discovered.

"I think she may still have been alive here," Inspector Robbins said. But there was little else to help him—or me— understand why this girl had to die.

He gestured to the road. "Walk with me back to the station. I'll need your statement."

I knew what was in his mind.

"I didn't kill her. I've never seen her before. But I'm her age. You aren't."

He laughed, a deep chuckle that reminded me of the Colonel Sahib, my father. We called him that when he was pompous.

We walked in silence past the houses that faced the water, and to where the shops began, heralding the center of

Eastbury. The police station was only a stone's throw from my hotel, a small hostelry that catered to off-season travelers like me.

I wrote out my statement and signed it, then passed it to the constable set to watch over me. And then Inspector Robbins was back again. "Would you care for a cup of tea, Miss Crawford?"

I thought he must have put in some telephone calls. His manner was very different. And I was as dry as the desert. So I accepted, to see what he was up to.

We sat down in a corner of the little shop where one could choose from the scant array of baked goods and take tea with friends. I wasn't sure Inspector Robbins was a friend. After he'd ordered jam-filled biscuits and tea, he turned back to me.

"Captain MacRae died of his wounds in Surrey. He was buried there five days ago. Sarah Elizabeth MacRae, his daughter, is missing."

The coast of Sussex was not so very far from Surrey.

"Why do they feel she's missing?"

"Because," he said, "she eloped against her parents' wishes. Her mother has sent for the police."

"*Eloped?*"

He relished my surprise. "Yes, you didn't foresee that, did you?"

Frowning, I said, "She didn't seem to be the sort…" I gave that some thought. "Was the Captain very rich, do you think?"

"What does that have to do with—oh, I see. Was she an heiress, worth cultivating and marrying?"

I said, "She looked so very young. Not just in age. Protected. Cosseted. Inexperienced."

"And you, of course, are elderly and wise?" He was making fun of me.

"I've seen more dead bodies than you ever have, Inspector. I've seen wounds that would make you turn away. I've held men down while their limbs were cut off. It takes away a little of your youth and innocence."

"I'm sorry," he said for the second time. And I thought he meant it. "It's just that I've never shared an inquiry with a young woman before. Young women don't belong in police work. It's a sordid business."

I smiled. "And so you want to send me back to my parents and tell them not to let me involve myself in murder. But I already have. I found her."

"And if she eloped without her parents' blessing and was cut off without a penny, perhaps the man who did this married her for her money, then killed her when he discovered he wouldn't see the fortune he was expecting."

"She was stabbed in the back," I said. "It could be that she'd already learned what an unscrupulous man he was. Possibly he was willing to wait a bit longer to see if her family changed their minds. But she was disillusioned, and wanted to go home. Annulments can be arranged."

"Hmmm. And I'll give you odds the man isn't local. I'll give you odds he thought the sea would take the body, and no one would be the wiser."

"She was in dry sand. He should have put her where it was wet." They had come with our tea, and I was feeling cold now. I sipped mine, warming my hands around the cup.

"I didn't think to ask the man's name. But that can be rectified. They would have been staying in a hotel. I'll send my men out to ask about."

"I don't think he—her killer—is still in Eastbury. Would you linger?" I asked Inspector Robbins. "And who was the woman who came down to the beach?"

"Someone who doesn't wish to be involved with the police."

"Or an accomplice, come to see if she was still there or not." I finished my second biscuit before I knew it. "Or perhaps she killed Sarah out of jealousy."

"I thought we were agreed that the husband or whatever he calls himself had killed her?" His smile reached his blue eyes this time.

"I'd question both of them, in your shoes."

He laughed again, that deep chuckle, so like my father's. "Has anyone ever suggested that nursing wasn't your true profession?"

"My mother, on any number of occasions."

"She's a wise woman, your mother." Finishing his tea, he said, "Well, pleasant as this has been, I have work to do."

"You won't leave me out of the picture here at the very end!" I demanded. "After I've been so much help to you."

He was standing now, and he hesitated. "Oh, very well. It won't hurt to find out more about our mysterious suitor."

We went back to the police station, and he put in another telephone call to Surrey. His eyes on me as he spoke, he agreed with several things being said to him, and then was busy writing something on a thick pad of paper.

I felt very out of place in this dingy room, down a dingier corridor from the main desk where a very grim old sergeant had glared at me for returning, as if once I'd given my statement, I was excess baggage to be collected only if the need arose.

Inspector Robbins put up the phone and looked at me quizzically. "Sarah's mother is coming to see if the body we found is indeed her daughter. I rather hope it isn't."

"So do I, except that we'd be no farther along. And I'd rather see her taken back where she belongs. She looked so— lost there on the beach."

"Very sentimental of you."

I could feel myself blushing. "And the man?"

"He and his sister—they tell me the woman is his sister— live in Hastings."

"Not very far from here," I said. "There's a much better strand there, but it's very close to the net drying sheds and the fishing boats. Even if they don't go out very often, it's a busy place."

"Know it, do you?"

"One of my flatmates has spent a summer there." I hesitated. "I brought my motorcar down from London. It's less noticeable than a police motorcar."

But he insisted that we use his transportation, and in the end, it was just as well.

As we were walking out to it, the doctor caught us up and said, "I was just coming to find you. That poor girl was stabbed with a pair of scissors."

Inspector Robbins looked at me, and then said to the doctor, "A very timely bit of information, sir."

Thanks to the Hastings police, we found the house where one Martin Worrel lived. And he was not there. His sister, a tall woman with pretty brown hair, informed us that he was in Oxford, staying with friends. She denied all knowledge of Sarah MacRae's whereabouts, saying that the girl had refused to go to Oxford with her brother, and the last they'd seen of her, Sarah MacRae was at the Hastings railway station, intent on returning home.

Glancing at the open sewing basket on a small table beneath the parlor window, I said, "What is your brother's birth date, Miss Worrel?"

She stared at me as if I'd grown horns.

"Miss Worrel?" Inspector Robbins had taken out his notebook and was referring to it as if the answer were written there.

She turned then and ran, shoving me aside and reaching the door to the front steps when a waiting constable stopped her. Whipping around, she raced toward the kitchen passage, and we heard the banging of doors as she went. But Inspector Robbins was a careful man. Another constable was waiting for her there, having slipped down the narrow alley between her house and the next. She was brought back in his grip, her face flushed with anger and fright.

She was taken into custody, to help with inquiries. The police in Oxford were searching for her brother. If that's what he was. There was a smooth spot on her ring finger where a wedding band would fit very well.

I had to leave for London the next morning, and I asked Inspector Robbins if he would keep me informed about the murder.

He promised, and there was a letter from him waiting for me on my next leave.

It said simply that Sarah and Martin had quarreled, presumably over the lost inheritance, and he'd stormed out, telling her to go home where she belonged. A lover's quarrel that might have blown over. His "sister," in fact his companion in crime, Lucy Edwards, had agreed to take Sarah MacRae to the railway station that evening. Instead, she'd stabbed her as she was packing her valise, driven the body to the churchyard in Eastbury, where she'd pulled on Martin's boots and carried Sarah out to the strand. That explained why the footprints weren't deeper—tall as she was, Lucy weighed far less than a man. She had been afraid that as lovers do, the two might make up. Sarah was very pretty for an heiress, and likely to be competition for Lucy. Inspector Robbins had also found the other earring. There was a strand of Sarah's hair still caught in it. Lucy had intended to keep both as profit, but lost one while carrying the dead girl.

And so Sarah had identified her murderer for us. That bit of paper—we never discovered how that followed her to the beach—and that earring had sealed Lucy Edwards' fate.

At the end of his letter, Inspector Robbins had written, "And how did you enjoy your role as a police consultant?"

I returned a humorous reply. The truth was, I had felt a kinship with Sarah MacRae. She wasn't just a girl dead on a beach and left for the tides to take her. Or an opportunity for me to play at policeman. Although I'd never known him, Captain MacRae had served in my father's old regiment—it was in that scrap of obituary I'd read. And so I had felt strong ties to him and to his daughter.

COLD COMFORT

An Inspector Ian Rutledge Story

It was hot this far down in the tunnel. Here, at the very end, there was only room for the three of them—Lieutenant Rutledge, the officer in charge; a private by the name of Williams at the left wall already passing over his bayonet in favor of a small knife as he scraped quietly at the chalk surface to enlarge the space; and Corporal MacLeod listening for sounds from the enemy burrowing their way toward the British lines in a counter tunnel, the stethoscope in his hand moving gently over the walls and ceiling. He glanced at Rutledge from time to time with a shake of his head.

Nothing.

It was an ominous silence.

A runner had just brought Rutledge the news that a German prisoner had been interrogated and there was the very real possibility that the enemy was working on its own tunnel, and that it could in fact parallel their own. If he was farther ahead, if he'd already packed his charges in his forward chamber, similar to the one that Rutledge and his men were still enlarging at their end, then chances were that the enemy's would go off first, burying the three of them alive.

The Germans had already used tunneling to fearful advantage. It was very simple: dig a tunnel that burrowed deep below No Man's Land to reach a spot beneath the British or French trenches opposite, then pack the final chamber with high explosives, set off the charges, and wreak shockingly effective havoc in the lines. And then launch an attack while one's opponent was still reeling. It was a variation of one of the favorite ways of breaching castle walls, something medieval armies had excelled at. Only instead of blowing up a trench, it weakened and brought down enough of the massive fortifications to allow the attacking army to rush inside. Dangerous work then, dangerous work now.

The Allies had had no choice but to use the same strategy as the Germans—and they were still learning. A team of miners from South Wales had been brought in because they were experienced men, capable of digging as well as shoring up the tunnel as they went.

The problem was, once the Welshmen were close enough to the German lines to be heard, picks and shovels had to be replaced by tedious, nearly silent scraping, inch by inch. Otherwise the enemy would hear them and take deadly countermeasures.

Rutledge had been sent down to relieve the officer in charge of the chamber, standing his eight-hour watch with his own corporal, Hamish MacLeod, whose hearing was particularly keen. And in place of the Welsh coal miners, Private Williams had been given the task of carrying on as quickly as he could without making a sound. He was a slate miner from North Wales, and it was clear several of the Welshmen from the South had resented the choice. He had been what was called a rock man, who drilled and set the explosives to bring down the great slabs of slate, and his touch was delicate. Fair for a Welshman, nearly as tall as Rutledge and MacLeod, he was a quiet man who kept to himself.

The knife picked away gently at the surface, filling the pail with surprising speed without a sound. The larger the chamber at the end of the tunnel, the more explosives that could be packed into it.

Two feet still to go, before the Royal Engineer overseeing the work would be satisfied.

All at once Hamish MacLeod held up a hand. Rutledge touched Williams' shoulder in the same instant. The Welsh private stopped, knife in midair, hardly breathing. Rutledge waited.

MacLeod took out a bit of paper, scribbled something on it, and handed it to Rutledge.

Not digging, it read. *Packing.*

The Germans must be worried that the prisoner had talked, and taking no chances, they were preparing to blow up their own tunnel as soon as possible, which meant they were already under the British lines. What MacLeod had heard was the soft footfalls of men carrying charges forward to stow in the already completed chamber.

Rutledge signaled to Williams and MacLeod to precede him back along the dark worm that was the British tunnel, and they carefully made their way to the main shaft.

Captain Marsh was standing there, a frown on his face. "Why have you stopped?"

"They're packing," Rutledge said. "We've got to hurry if we're to set off our charges before they finish and set off theirs."

"Damn," Marsh said. "Are you quite sure? There's no time to send for the Royal Engineers to verify this."

MacLeod stood his ground, holding up the stethoscope. "I'm sure," he replied.

"I don't trust those things," Marsh snapped, considering the young Scot. "The old pan-of-water system was more reliable. When the water *moved*, you knew for certain."

"Nevertheless," Rutledge said, "the runner warned us that the Germans were ahead of us." If Captain Marsh refused to believe Corporal MacLeod, or sent them back to the unfinished chamber while he consulted the Royal Engineers, then Rutledge and his two men would be the first to die as they frantically worked at the walls. If the explosion didn't kill them outright, they would be buried alive and then slowly suffocate.

"Yes, all right." Marsh looked up the shaft, calling softly to the men waiting there.

It was a matter of minutes before the charges were being brought down. Five men followed, carrying them barefooted down the tunnel to the end. Williams, eyes narrowed, watched them go.

"I'll set the fuse," he offered, a little too casually.

And Rutledge, who had been an inspector at Scotland Yard before the war had begun, in 1914, had the strongest feeling that the man didn't trust a coal miner to do the work properly. The question was, *why*? Private Lloyd and Private Jones had been chosen because they were experienced men.

His time at the Yard now seemed like years ago, not just a matter of months. Still, dealing with murder inquiries, he'd learned to trust his feelings, his instincts. And something about the way Williams had spoken had caught his attention.

Marsh went back down the tunnel, overseeing the placing of the charges. It would be a full load, and by the time the space at the end was packed and the bags of chalk were piled against the charges to make sure the blast was contained and didn't blow back into the British lines, the Germans might well catch them all like rats in a hole. A risky business, but they all knew that.

Rutledge stood to one side, cautioning the men passing the charges to mind what they were about and to be as quiet as possible. Twice he saw the one of the miners glare at Williams, but whatever the problem was, it would have to wait.

When the last charge had been laid, the bags of chalk were taken down and packed tight, and then it was only a matter of setting off the blast. Williams collected his gear and prepared to connect the fuse to the blasting caps.

But Marsh didn't send for Williams.

Instead, it was Private Lloyd who set the fuse. The last man out, he came racing down the tunnel, grinning broadly as he passed Williams.

Everyone scrambled up the shaft, out of harm's way, grateful for the night that covered their movements. The sector closest to them had kept up a desultory fire, to be sure the Germans were well occupied, and the rifle flashes lit No Man's Land with brief bursts of brightness.

The caps were crimped onto the fuse and set off.

The seconds ticked away.

Rutledge glanced at his watch, counting them.

The fuse should have reached the charges by now. Standing beside him, Marsh stirred, well aware of time passing.

"It was all right," he said. "Private Lloyd set it, while Private Jones stood by. They're good men."

But blasting caps could be uncertain. The crimp at the fuse could be bad. The fuse could have gone out for any number of reasons.

Rutledge checked the caps. They appeared to have worked.

"Why didn't you summon Williams?" he asked over his shoulder as Marsh watched him.

"Time was short. Lloyd said he could deal with it. He and Jones. They've done it before."

Rutledge straightened, turned and walked toward the tunnel shaft. "There's no time to discuss it. The fuse has to be checked."

Any delay meant that the German tunnel would blow first. And no one was precisely sure where under the line of British trenches it ended.

Captain Marsh peered around in the darkness. "Lloyd? Where are you?"

"He's gone to the latrines," someone answered. Rutledge thought it was Private Jones, but he couldn't be certain where the voice had come from

"Williams, then," Marsh pointed to him. "Go with Rutledge, man."

Rutledge took the bulky stethoscope from MacLeod, who was protesting, saying he should be the one to go, but Rutledge shook his head and was already letting himself down the shaft, not waiting for Marsh or Williams.

The two men, officer and private soldier, bent their heads and ran down the tunnel, not worrying about noise until they were within twenty feet of the chalk barricade. Slowing, the two men crept forward, Rutledge's torch searching for the fuse.

"It's gone under the bags of chalk," Williams said in a whisper. "Look."

They stopped short. The fuse had burned to this point. Was it still lit? Or had it gone out, accidentally snuffed by the lack of air or the weight of the barrier?

Rutledge could feel the cold sweat breaking out as he stepped cautiously over the fuse and knelt by the sacking just above it. Hearing only his own heart beat as he put the stethoscope in his ears, he pressed the bell against the lumpy chalk surface and listened.

The fuse was still burning.

And there was no telling now how much time was left.

"Run!" He was already on his way, Williams ahead of him, both men silently counting off the distance to safety. They had barely reached the shaft, out of breath and already grabbing at the ropes, when the air seemed to be sucked out of the space around them, and the charges blew.

The ground shook beneath their feet, and across No Man's Land, a vast plume of earth rose high in the air then rained down like black sleet. Rutledge could hear it even as he threw himself to one side, but Williams was caught in the ropes, dangling like a puppet.

And then Captain Marsh was there, pulling Williams up, shouting to Rutledge. In that same instant, the German charges blew, shattering the night with their thunder as a second plume of earth went straight up, blotting out the stars, this time tearing apart half a sector of the British line and finishing off the British tunnel.

There would be no charge tonight across No Man's Land to follow up at the weakest point of the line, where the tunnel had torn apart its defenses. The damage on both sides was too great.

The Welsh miners and their officers, Rutledge among them, lay where they'd fallen, dazed, half deaf, covered in the stinking earth, and then they were scrambling to their feet, racing for the trenches to pull out the British wounded and dead. Men had been tossed every which way, some of them still unaware they'd been hurt, others deafened or stunned by the shock waves, staring up at their rescuers with blank eyes.

It was five hours later, the wounded dealt with, the dead carried out, repair work already underway in the damaged line of trenches, when Rutledge collected Corporal MacLeod, Captain Marsh, and Private Williams, then sent for Privates Jones and Lloyd. They went to stand at the head of what had once been the shaft to the blown tunnel.

He was very angry as he faced them. Captain Marsh had already refused to lay the blame at anyone's door, insisting that fuses and explosives were undependable down in the tunnels, that delays had occurred before.

But Rutledge wasn't satisfied. Too many men had died to sweep the delay under the proverbial rug. And he was determined to get to the bottom of what had happened on his watch.

"That fuse was too long," he said. "As a result, it allowed the Germans to set theirs, and fire their own charges. We lost good men because of it. They weren't sappers, they were *my* men, in *my* sector. I want to know what went wrong."

Marsh cleared his throat, shifting from one foot to the other. Rutledge grimly waited for someone to answer him.

"It was the right length," Private Jones said finally. "I was present when Aaron—Private Lloyd—cut it. And I saw him crimp the fuse to the caps. It was done the way it should be."

Private Lloyd stared straight at Rutledge. "There must have been a problem with dampness. Sir."

The two Welshmen were very much alike, dark haired, dark eyed, broad shouldered from years in the collieries, coal dust still deeply ingrained in their faces and hands. Lloyd, the handsomer of the two, possessed a cockiness that bordered on insolence, only just falling short of defiance.

"It was three minutes late," Rutledge retorted. "It was still burning as Williams and I reached the chalk bags. It should have gone off well ahead of the German trench. It should have smothered their fuse."

"It was the right length," Lloyd repeated stubbornly. "I knew what I was about."

Captain Marsh interrupted. "It comes down to my fault. I didn't check it. We were working against the clock. It *looked* all right."

Williams couldn't keep quiet any longer. "We were nearly killed. Lieutenant Rutledge and me. We shouldn't have had to go down there once it was lit."

Private Jones glared at him. "I tell you, the fuse was all right. Private Lloyd here knows what he's about. We measured *right*."

It was the word of Private Jones against Rutledge's own observations. And it was true, they had had to work in haste.

There was something he ought to remember about these two men, Lloyd and Jones. But he was tired and it escaped him. Something he'd been told by the officer who had brought them up to the front lines.

He said, "Captain Marsh?" Hoping his superior officer would back him up.

But he didn't. Marsh had no experience with explosives, only the tunneling itself. "We were unlucky," he said finally. "The Germans were farther along than we knew. I'm sure that's the answer."

Fighting to bottle up his anger, Rutledge said, "I don't believe it is." He turned and walked back to the lines and his sector. He realized halfway there that Private Williams had followed him. He slowed so that Corporal MacLeod could precede him.

When the young Scot was out of hearing, Rutledge stopped and turned. Williams stopped as well.

"I think they were trying to kill me," the man said quietly, glancing over his shoulder to be certain they were alone. "Lloyd and his half-brother Jones."

That's what he'd been trying to remember. The two Welshmen were half-brothers.

The officer had pointed this out, mentioning that they had insisted on serving together. It wasn't uncommon for entire villages or men from large estates to insist on serving side by side. But in this case, it made a difference.

Whether the fuse was long or short, it was likely that Lloyd and Jones would stand up for each other in a crisis.

"Why?" Rutledge snapped. "Why did they intend to kill you?"

If Williams was right, he, Rutledge, was dealing with cold—blooded murder. Of the men in the trenches, and nearly of Williams and himself. What kind of hate, he wondered fleetingly, could account for so much killing?

For an instant, he felt himself back at the Yard, questioning a witness. Only there, he faced only his chief superintendent's wrath, not German rifle fire. He smiled grimly to himself at the thought as shots stitched the trench wall just inside the barbed wire that protected it.

"They don't believe I'm a slate man. Or that I come from the slate mines below Mount Snowdon. They think I was one of the clay kickers from Manchester. The men who were digging the sewers."

"Why should it matter?"

"I don't know." Williams shrugged. "This isn't the first time they've attacked me."

"What do you mean?"

Shelling had commenced, now, first from the German lines, probing shots along the sector with the damaged trenches, and then answering bombardment from the British lines.

Rutledge sprinted for the safety of the trench wall, and Williams followed.

"It was on the train, coming up from Calais," he said breathlessly, as earth from the shelling rained down on them. "I was tripped, and when I went down, I was hit hard and kicked. It was Lloyd, I'd swear to it. And Jones didn't try to stop him. Someone else had to step in. Marching toward the Front, someone—I never saw who it was, but I can guess—shoved me into the path of a lorry. If the driver hadn't swerved just in time, I'd have been run down. Add to that, this is the second time I've been faced with a long fuse." He shrugged again, his face shadowed by his helmet.

"Are you sure it's the same men?"

"Yes, two of the Cardiff miners. Taffy Jones and Aaron Lloyd had seen to the fuse that time too."

"Then why did you go back down that tunnel with me? If you knew they'd done this before?"

"Because I wanted to see for myself what had happened. I never made it as far as the chalk face that other time. Captain Marsh had to dig me out. I had nothing to show for being half buried alive except suspicion."

Rutledge nodded. "All right. I'll see what I can discover."

Later, as they kept watch in the middle of the night, Rutledge told Corporal Hamish MacLeod what he'd learned from Williams. The young Scot was steady, good with his men, and observant. Rutledge had come to trust him.

"Did they know each other before they came to France?" He passed the periscope to Rutledge, whose turn it was to look over the lip of the trench without attracting the attention of any waiting sniper. "The three Welshmen?"

"I don't believe they did." The night was quiet after the barrage.

"It's a puzzle," MacLeod said. "The question is, how could they be sure it would ha' been Williams who went back down the tunnel?"

"Because he should have been the one to set the fuse. And because he was sent back the last time it was too long. His responsibility." Rutledge considered the question. "And because Lloyd wasn't there. He'd gone to the latrines."

"Aye. Verra' convenient, that. Ye ken, if it was on purpose, yon long fuse, they didna' care if you'd died along with Williams."

"Whatever their reason for wanting to kill Williams, it has to run deep." He shook his head. "The problem is, there's nothing we can do until there's more solid evidence. I can only hope Williams survives that long."

But nothing happened to Williams when the next tunnel was set off. Or the next. Rutledge was there, keeping an eye on what was being done.

It was nearly a week after that, toward midnight, when Private Williams was found lying in a pool of blood and half dead.

The soldier who discovered him, Private MacRae, a Scot from Stirling, reported to Rutledge after seeing Williams back to a forward aid station.

"Rumor says he was careless and a sniper got him. But we havna' had a sniper this fortnight."

"Rumor . . . was there a name attached to that rumor?"

"It was a Welshman. He was at yon aid station, suffering from a boil on his foot. He said Williams was too tall for a Welshman, and the sniper found an easy target."

Rutledge considered what Private MacRae had said. *Too tall for a Welshman. . .*

It was true, Williams could give Jones and the rest of the South Wales miners a good three inches. Sturdy men, compactly built, darker. Williams had a leaner, thinner build, and his hair was lighter. Was that why some of the miners thought he must be from Manchester? Or had Jones and Lloyd started that lie?

But coming from Manchester—or any other English town where industry thrived—was hardly a reason for murder.

"What was the name of the Welshman, do you know?"

MacRae shook his head. "I didna' think to ask."

On his next rotation a few days later, Rutledge went behind the British lines to look for Private Williams. He was still in hospital, the shot having missed his lung but damaged his shoulder. Bound up with his left arm braced in the air like the broken wing of an aircraft, Williams lay back against his pillows with the lined face of a man in pain.

"A very little bit lower, sir, and I'd have been done for," he said, as Rutledge sat down in the chair by his bed and asked how he felt.

"I've just spoken to the doctor," Rutledge replied. "He tells me the bullet entered from the back. Not the front. This wasn't a sniper's work."

"I don't know who it was. I didn't see anyone. I was coming back from the shaft we'd been digging. It was dark, quiet. And I felt the shot before I heard it. It spun me around and still I didn't see anyone."

Rutledge found that part hard to believe. Williams must have glimpsed the man. And even if he weren't positive, he must have had his suspicions.

"You aren't planning on a little private revenge, are you? This is an Army matter. Let the Army deal with it."

"I'm tired of being hunted, sir. That's all."

"The doctor has reported the wound as suspicious. It will be investigated."

"Yes, well, that may be." He turned his head away so that Rutledge couldn't see his eyes. "He'll claim—whoever he is— that he was cleaning his rifle. And he'll have a witness, you can be sure of it." His voice was bitter.

"All the same, I'll have a word with Jones and his half-brother."

Williams smiled without humor. "Good luck to you, then. Sir."

Back in the line again, Rutledge found Captain Marsh during a lull in the fighting and asked permission to speak to the Welsh miners.

Marsh shook his head. "They've been sent back. We've got Griffiths's clay kickers now. They know what they're about. No fuse problems since they took over the task."

"When were the miners sent back?" Rutledge asked sharply.

"Yesterday morning." He shook his head. "Two had to be dropped off at the base hospital. A nuisance, that. One had a shell splinter that wouldn't heal, he said, and the other had a broken toe. I don't know where the other miners will be posted next. Where they're needed, I expect."

"Did you examine these wounds?"

"There was no time. The Sisters will sort them out."

"Who were these wounded men?"

"Privates Jones and Lloyd." Marsh frowned. "Look, Rutledge, what's this about? What have you got against those two? They didn't shoot themselves in the foot, you know. They had a legitimate reason for stopping by the base hospital."

He had his answer.

The base hospital for this sector was where Private Williams was being treated. And if Jones and Lloyd intended to finish what they'd begun, this was very likely their last chance.

The Germans attacked five minutes later, and a vicious defense was all that kept the British line from folding. Rutledge, encouraging his own men, held his sector, and managed to rally men down the line as the Germans breached the barbed wire, firing down into the trenches and tossing grenades as soon as they'd come within range. When the British machine gun, which had jammed, had been cleared and opened up again, it turned the tide, and the German advance became a shambling retreat.

Relieved to find they had fewer dead than he'd expected, Corporal MacLeod, set about collecting the wounded.

He pointed to Rutledge's roughly bandaged arm. "Ye'll need that attended to as well."

"I can't leave. Not until I've been relieved."

"Aye, and ye'll be down with the gangrene, wait and see."

Later, when the relief column came down the line, Rutledge went back to the nearest aid station to look in on his wounded men.

The doctor insisted on treating him as well. Examining Rutledge's arm, the doctor looked up. "You're lucky that shot didn't sever the artery. You're out of the line for three days."

His men were in rotation, in the reserve trenches where they could lick their wounds and rest. They were safe enough. It was his chance. "I'd like to visit a soldier sent back to the base hospital. Can you arrange it?"

"You should be resting. Still—if you'll ask one of the Sisters to see to clean bandages tomorrow, and you don't exert yourself unduly and start with a fever, I see no harm in it."

"I give you my word."

There was room in one of the ambulances heading south with the next contingent of wounded. Rutledge took a seat next to the driver. The man smelled of wine, and glad to have an audience, he launched into a long monologue, never pausing as he rambled from one thought to the next. He was from Leeds, he said, a baker before the war, and he hated France.

Rutledge, left to his own thoughts, wondered if he was making too much of the danger to Williams. Now that he was on his way to the base hospital, nursing his aching arm as the ambulance bounced and slid through the ruts, he told himself that the orderlies and Sisters were the only protection Williams needed. Killing someone in full view of so many witnesses was different from shooting someone in the back. What's more, Williams wouldn't be leaving the hospital anytime soon. He wasn't likely to encounter either Jones or Lloyd even when he did, for they would be reassigned elsewhere.

Then why, Rutledge asked himself, did he feel such a sense of urgency?

Just then the driver said something that brought his mind sharply back to the rambling soliloquy.

"I'm sorry—what was it you were saying?"

But the driver took exception to Rutledge's sudden interest. He retorted gruffly, "I shouldn't have told you—"

"But you did. You said you were given a choice between prison and enlisting. Since your lungs weren't good enough, you had no choice but to drive an ambulance."

"What if I did?" he asked sullenly.

"Before that. Why was it you were brought up on charges?"

"I told you."

"Tell me again. Or I'll report you for drinking and ignoring your patients back there."

"All right, then, you needn't cut up stiff over it. I tried to kill a man. But he lived."

"Who was the man?"

"He was a trades union man. He caught my brother when he tried to cross the strike line and go back to work. Fred needed the pay, he couldn't afford to be out on strike."

"Where was this strike?"

Goaded the man said, "What are you, a copper? Why does it matter?"

"Was it in England—or was it a colliery in Wales?"

"Of course it wasn't Wales, it was in Lancashire. The trades union men beat him nearly senseless. And the doctors said they couldn't do anything for him. He died the next morning. He was a good man, and he left a wife and three little 'uns. Tell me that's fair?"

"It isn't fair. But neither is attempted murder. Were they brought up on charges? The men who did this to your brother?"

"There was no one who could identify them. No one saw anything," the driver said bitterly and turned his attention to what passed for the road. They traveled in silence for the rest of the journey.

Rutledge found Williams sitting on the side of his cot this time, trying to manage to spoon up the dinner he'd been brought.

Taking the chair from the next bed and sitting down, Rutledge greeted him and then said, "Are you a trades union man?"

Williams stopped, the spoon half way to his mouth. "Am I *what*?"

Rutledge repeated the question.

Shaking his head vehemently, Williams said, "No, by God, I'm not. Sir."

"I suspect Jones and his friends think you are."

Williams stared at him. "I'll be damned. But why?"

"I don't know. It could be the reason they've tried to kill you. There's bad blood on both sides of that fight. Men have been murdered. And *Williams* is a common-enough name in Wales and in England. You could have lied about your background at the slate mines."

"I haven't. But there's no way to prove it, short of sending to the manager of the mine."

"The coal miners have been moved back from the Front. Griffiths has brought in some of his clay kickers, men building the Manchester sewers. More to the point, at least two of the coal miners were on their way *here*, to the base hospital. Lloyd and Jones. It may be a coincidence, and it may not. Watch yourself. You're in no condition to do battle with anyone."

"There's truth to that, God knows." Williams realized he was still holding his spoon in midair, and he set it down carefully. "I don't like this."

"Then tell me what you saw that night, when you were shot. Let me charge whoever did this." Rutledge gestured to the bound shoulder.

"My word against theirs? No, it won't save me. Can I be moved to another hospital?"

"By the time the paperwork is completed, it could be too late. I'll see if I can persuade Matron to put you on the next convoy to England."

But Matron shook her head after Rutledge had made his request. "We have far more serious cases than this one. Private Williams is healing well. I can't justify sending him back."

"His life could be in danger, if he stays here."

"Surely you exaggerate, Lieutenant. We've had no trouble at this hospital. The men who are here need care, and there's no time for or thought of private quarrels." She looked at a list. "What's more, I don't even have a record of the two men you've mentioned. Private Aaron Lloyd, Private Taffy Jones. It could be that you are entirely mistaken."

But she didn't know Private Lloyd or his half-brother. It was worrying that they hadn't been treated yet—where were they? And Williams' willingness to believe in the danger facing him was further proof that he wasn't satisfied that the two Welshmen had finished with him.

Rutledge went to have a final word with Williams. "Matron won't consider England. Still, I've warned the Sister in charge of this ward that you have enemies. It's the best I can do. I've also asked one of the orderlies to watch for Lloyd and Jones, and report to Matron. It's possible they won't turn up here, that they're waiting for you come to them. I wouldn't go walking far, if Sister asks you to start exercising your legs again."

"I'm grateful, sir. Truly I am."

Rutledge stayed at the base hospital another day, walking through the wards, speaking to the patients, keeping an eye open for Private Jones and Private Lloyd. On the third day, his ambulance was set to leave for the Front and he had no choice but to be aboard, if he was to rejoin his company.

He spoke to Williams a last time, and five minutes later he was settling himself in the uncomfortable seat beside a different driver when he heard a commotion in the ward he'd just left.

"Wait for me," he ordered the man as he got out and sprinted back the way he'd come.

He found a Sister bleeding from a blow to the face, and down the ward, where Williams had been lying just minutes before, he could see an overturned chair and bedclothes dragged out into the aisle. Men were sitting up in their cots, shouting to Rutledge, pointing back the way he'd just come.

He bent over the Sister, asking her, "What happened here?"

"Two men—they took away Private Williams. I couldn't see their faces. They were wearing hospital masks. I don't know where they've taken him."

He shouted for help, but didn't stay to explain to the staff rushing to the Sister's aid, his mind already busy with the problem of where the three men might be. Had his own presence at the hospital precipitated this attack? Or the fact that he was seen to be leaving?

And then he heard one of the ambulances roaring into life, men shouting, and someone firing a shot.

He raced toward the line of ambulances he'd just left, saw his driver lying on the ground, dazedly trying to raise himself on his elbow. An orderly was already kneeling beside him. Rutledge ran on to the second ambulance in the line and called to the driver, "We've got to stop them."

But the driver leapt out of his door, shaking his head. "They've got a weapon."

Rutledge took his place behind the wheel, gunned the motor, and pulled out of line, turning in the direction of the fleeing ambulance heading fast toward the main road to Calais.

The ground was wet from recent rains, and he could feel his tires slipping and sliding in the viscous mud. Holding grimly to the wheel, he drove as fast as he dared, and then, when he saw he was making no headway, faster than was safe.

He was gaining, even as the ambulance bucketed across what passed for a road, narrowly missing a column of men marching toward the Front. He could hear the big guns behind him, opening up for another punishing marathon of shelling. And then the ambulance ahead of him skidded wildly, spun around, and missed a yawning ditch by inches. The driver got control again, but it had given Rutledge his chance. Praying that the tires would hold, he rammed his foot down on the accelerator and came up even with the fleeing vehicle.

Someone swung open one of the rear doors, and Rutledge could see Private Lloyd kneeling there. Behind him lay Williams. Lloyd was raising a revolver, pointing it toward Rutledge. But Williams somehow managed to use the rigid brace on his shoulder to spoil the man's aim just as he fired. Furious, the man backhanded him, sending Williams hard against the metal side of the ambulance, just as Rutledge sped past, cut in front of the vehicle, and forced it into the low wall that was all that was left of what had been the approach to a French barn.

The ambulance hit the wall at speed and came to a jarring stop, throwing Private Jones, the driver, into the wheel and then the windscreen. By the time Rutledge had braked and got out, he could see blood running down Jones's face. But it was the man with that revolver who was his main target.

He ran to the back of the ambulance and flung open both doors. Williams and Lloyd lay on the floor in a jumble of legs and arms.

Rutledge could hear another vehicle coming after him, but there was no time to wait. He climbed into the ambulance and pulled the unconscious Williams out, setting him against the stone wall. And then he went back for the armed man.

But Private Aaron Lloyd had broken his neck in the crash, his head striking the metal rim of the upper berths that held stretchers in place. He lay where he'd fallen, the revolver still clutched in his hand.

Leaving him, Rutledge went to look at the driver. Jones was badly hurt but alive, his nose and cheekbones broken by the impact with the windscreen.

"What the hell were you trying to do?" Rutledge demanded, pulling him from behind the wheel and leaning him against a wing. "Was it worth it, this abduction? Your half-brother is dead!"

"Williams ran off with my wife," Jones tried to answer, his voice muffled by his bleeding nose. "Then he left her in Manchester to die penniless and alone."

"Was he a trades union man? This Williams?"

"Aaron thought it likely. He came to the village where Sarah was staying with her sister. There was trouble with the colliery owner, and the man had to get out. When he left, Sarah went with him." He closed his eyes. "Williams was the right man. I swear he was. My brother told me. He recognized the bastard."

"Williams is a slate man. From North Wales. He had nothing to do with your wife." Rutledge was watching the approaching ambulance come to rescue them. "Your brother lied to you."

"Aaron never lies. Williams is from Manchester."

"Then why didn't Lloyd try to stop Sarah—or call you to come to Manchester to fetch her back? Where was he all this time, watching and doing nothing, letting her die alone?"

Jones stared at him through bloodshot eyes. "He said he tried. He said he even followed them to Manchester, but Sarah wouldn't listen."

"Apparently Aaron was a great one for *saying*. Where was *he*?"

"He was ill, bad lungs. He was sent away to recover. Away from the coal dust." After a moment he added unwillingly, "To the same village. That's how he knew."

"And he didn't warn you? He didn't summon you to come and put a stop to whatever Williams was up to?"

The man's gaze went to the open doors at the rear of the ambulance. He couldn't see his brother's body from where he lay. He made to get up, and Rutledge shoved him back down. "He said—" Taffy Jones began again.

"Why weren't you holding the revolver on Williams? Why was it Aaron? She was your wife. You should have shot him."

"He said I had no stomach for what had to be done. It's one thing to be killing Germans. The blood's up. I'd failed twice, when it came down to it. He said he'd see to it. Are you certain he's dead? I don't believe you."

"Don't you understand, you fool? I'd wager it was Aaron who ran off with your wife. Abandoned her when he had finished with her. And she was too shamed to come home again. Why else would he have been in the back of the ambulance, with the weapon? He didn't want you to confront Williams. To listen to him. Why was he so insistent that Williams had to die? She was *your* wife, not his."

Jones roused himself, putting a hand up to his nose and eyes. As if to fend off what Rutledge was saying.

"He wouldn't do such a thing. You're lying."

"He tried to persuade you to kill an innocent man. For all I know, it was Aaron who shot Williams in the back—for *you. Your* revenge."

In spite of the bloody mask that was Jones' face, Rutledge could read his eyes. "It's true, then. Bloody cowards, both of you," he said in disgust.

"He told me he was a better shot. Doing it in cold blood."

The other ambulance had caught up with them. An orderly jumped out and ran to Jones, then peered into the back of the stolen vehicle. Another came to kneel beside Williams, still lying against the wall but just regaining consciousness.

A third was demanding to know what had happened.

As Rutledge got to his feet, Jones tried to shake his head but was in too much pain. "I won't believe you. Not until I've spoken to Aaron."

"Believe what?" the orderly demanded. "Sir, we need to get these men to hospital. And what am I to do about that ambulance?"

Rutledge moved back. "I'll explain later. Just now I want this man to be held under guard for attempted murder. There will be other charges, but that will do for now."

The orderly lifted Jones to his feet. Jones looked up at Rutledge. Something stirred in his eyes. And then he lashed out at the man holding his arm.

Rutledge swore as the wounded man broke free of the orderly's grip and stumbled toward the back of the ambulance. He held on to the doors and leaned in, peering at his brother's body. "He wouldn't have lied to me," he insisted, his voice heavy with grief and pain. "Not Aaron. Not about Sarah."

Rutledge pointed to the revolver. "Where did he get this?"

"He took it from a dead officer. He couldn't find Williams in Manchester—he thought the bastard might be in France. And he was. Family honor, Aaron said." Jones put up a hand and wiped at the blood on his face. "I loved her. I never thought she'd betray me. But when I looked at Williams, it all made sense. She always did have an eye for tall men."

"Lloyd must have been afraid that you'd find out the truth and go after him instead. And so he tried to persuade you to kill an innocent man. That's the only thing that makes sense. Family honor indeed."

"He'd never lied to me before."

"Have you asked Sarah's sister? Did she describe Williams?"

"Aaron spoke to her. He said. I was down the mines, you see. I couldn't go. But he could. What with the pneumonia."

"You're a fool," Rutledge said again. "For all you know, Sarah is still in Manchester, waiting for your half-brother to come back from the war. You have only Lloyd's word that any of this happened, and under the circumstances, I'd not trust anything he said. And if Williams was killed, you'd have hanged for it. Not Aaron. Didn't it occur to you that if the Germans didn't shoot you, your own side would? For murder? Cheaper than a divorce."

Jones lunged at Rutledge, but the orderly caught him and this time held him.

Leaving them, Rutledge went to search the pockets of the dead man, and stopped, staring at something he'd just pulled out of Lloyd's tunic.

Stepping out of the ambulance again, he held what he'd found out for Jones to see.

It was a letter. It didn't require a policeman to realize that Jones recognized the writing. He also recognized the name on the envelope. *Private Aaron Lloyd.*

Jones snatched the letter from Rutledge's hand. Pulling the sheets out of the envelope, he unfolded them and started to read. Halfway through, he crumpled the pages in his fist.

"He told me she was dead! Buried in a pauper's grave."

Without warning, he reached into the ambulance, took the revolver from his half-brother's dead hand, and before Rutledge could stop him, he fired three shots point blank into Aaron Lloyd's inert body.

And then he dropped the weapon and meekly followed the orderly to the waiting ambulance. Stepping inside, he sank into the nearest cot, his hands shaking.

Rutledge bent down to retrieve the discarded letter.

It had been written only three weeks before. The first paragraph told him enough.

> *My darling Aaron,*
>
> *Is it over yet? Please tell me Taffy is dead and that other man as well. And that you are safe, and will come home to me soon. I beg you to take care of yourself and let nothing happen to you. I couldn't bear it . . .*

Rutledge folded the letter and returned it to the envelope. He'd been right about Aaron Lloyd. But it gave him no satisfaction. Still, the letter could be entered into evidence when Jones was tried as an accomplice to attempted murder.

Williams, shaking his head as the second orderly tried to help him back to the same ambulance, said, "No. I won't ride with that bloody man, Jones. Not after what he did." And then to Rutledge he said, "Private Lloyd intended to kill me as soon as we were clear of the hospital. 'Boyo,' he said, 'it's a bit of bad luck for you, but the only way out for me.' Cold comfort, that."

THE MAHARANI'S PEARLS

A Bess Crawford Story

British Army Garrison, Northern India,
when Bess Crawford was ten

"BESS, FOR GOD'S sake, what are you doing?"

It was my father's batman—his Army servant—standing in the tent opening. I was sitting cross—legged on the dusty carpet, and the fortune—teller had just finished spreading out her cards.

"Simon, please! I want to hear what she has to say."

"And your mother will have my head if I don't bring you back to tea *now*."

"Pretend you haven't found me—keep looking for another few minutes. *Please*?" I begged. "I know I must change before the Maharani arrives. It would never do to appear for tea looking as if I'd just come from the bazaar. But there's still plenty of time."

"You *will* have just come from the bazaar. She arrived early. And you'll have fleas before you leave, if not worse." He pointed to the dog lying behind the fortune-teller, busy scratching its shoulder.

If the Maharani had just arrived, it would be at least another half hour before tea was brought in.

"Simon—"

"I'll be cashiered, Bess."

"Shhhh. It will only take another moment or two," I begged, then I turned back to the fortune-teller and said in Hindi, "Continue. But hurry, please."

She bent over the cards, frowning. "You will be in danger on the water," she said in that singsong voice that gave the impression she was in a trance. But she wasn't. It was part of the show one pays for when one has one's fortune told. "And I see a great conflict, not now, but to come."

So far her guesses were on the mark. I was English, and there was always danger on the water as we took ship to and from home. As for a great conflict, my father was a British Army officer. War was his business, great or small.

Simon, still in the doorway, said again, in a voice that brooked no argument. "Elizabeth."

I said to the fortune-teller, "Quickly! Who will I marry? And will I be happy?"

But her face had changed as she studied the tattered cards spread across the space between us.

"The life of someone you care for is in grave danger. My child, you must go now. Before it is too late."

Simon's life, for not bringing me posthaste to tea? She must have understood what he'd been saying to me. It wasn't among his duties to play nanny to my father's daughter, but occasionally it was necessary for someone to look for me when I strayed to the horse lines, the bazaar, the temples, and all the other far more exciting places than our quiet garden, and lost track of the time. It certainly wasn't going to be my governess. Miss Stewart would have the vapors if she saw me now.

She didn't care for India very much. I suspected she'd come out to find a husband, and had taken a position as governess when she failed to meet a young man to her liking. She wouldn't be the first young Englishwoman to do so. When we left for England on my father's next leave, she would very likely go with us, and remain in London rather than travel back with us.

I thanked the fortune-teller, disappointed. I hadn't expected truth and wisdom, but I'd hoped for something I could write about to friends who had been sent back to school in England. Half our native staff went to fortune-tellers and believed in them. I had it on the authority of my *ayah*, the nursery-room maid, that this woman was the best.

I got up and walked to the tent opening, put out with Simon for spoiling my adventure. I said crossly, "I thought you and I were friends."

"So we are," he said, clearing a path for me past the snake charmer and the man eating fire. "But I have a duty to your father, and by extension, to your mother. You should have guessed the Maharani would arrive early. She often does. You could have asked me to take you to a fortune-teller tomorrow." He pushed aside a sacred cow meandering through the crowded marketplace, and caught my arm before I could pause to watch the man climbing a rope to nowhere.

"I *could* have asked," I said, "but I knew very well you'd have said no. So I came on my own."

Exasperated, he said, "Bess, you aren't safe wandering about a village by yourself. You're an English girl, your father is an officer. You could be abducted, held for ransom. Worse."

"In the last village where we lived, yes, I know. But here everyone is friendly. I'm not in any danger. Someone would come to my rescue. Besides, I brought my syce." My native groom was holding our horses on the outskirts of the village.

Simon shook his head in disgust. "Much good he would be."

I looked up at my companion. He was tall, and my mother said he was still growing. He'd come to us a recalcitrant, stubborn boy, having lied about his age to join the British Army, and nearly found himself in a cell before he'd been here six months. My father, seeing more in the rebellious boy than others had, made him his servant and set about taming him. Simon, he soon discovered, had come from a very good family and had been well educated. What had sent him haring off to become a soldier I didn't know, but I'd grown so accustomed to having him underfoot and keeping an eye on me when my father was busy that he was now almost a member of the family. In fact I could barely remember a time when he wasn't there. Sometimes I saw my father treating Simon as the son he'd never had. I wanted to be jealous, but I liked Simon too much to feel anything but relief that he hadn't been court-martialed and shot before my father took an interest in him. He'd saved me from countless escapades that might have incurred the wrath of my mother and he sometimes had been my co-conspirator in mischief as well.

But not today.

Simon had left his own mount with my syce, and as he gave me a foot up to my saddle, he told the groom what he thought of him for allowing me to come to the village without a proper escort.

The syce listened soberly, but when Simon's back was turned, gave me a sheepish smile that said he forgave me for getting him into trouble.

We trotted back to the cantonment, Simon smuggled me in through the kitchen, and my *ayah*, my nurse, was waiting, scolding me as she led me to my room. My clothes were laid out on the bed, and I bathed my face and hands, put them on quickly, and stood still while the *ayah* brushed out my long hair, bringing out the red-gold strands that kept it from being a mousy light brown.

She stood back to take a long look at me. "You'll do," she told me in Hindi. "Now quickly before the governess woman comes to find you."

I hurried down the passage, took a deep breath at the door to what would have been called a small drawing room in England, and tapped lightly before opening it.

"There you are," my mother said brightly, and I knew then she'd had to send Simon to find me—he hadn't come on his own.

The Maharani smiled at me as I curtsied. "Come and embrace me, child. Are you feverish? Your cheeks are pink."

I'd been hurrying, but I couldn't tell her that. "A touch of sun. I went riding this morning."

"Without your bonnet? My dear, you must remember you aren't used to this sun."

She was an old friend of my father's, her husband one of the strongest supporters of the British presence in his state. Forward thinking and intelligent, the Maharajah had tried to modernize his lands and introduce prosperity to his people, measures not always popular with his fellow princes or some members of his own family.

Tea was brought in and the conversation became general. But I could sense that before I'd arrived, the Maharani and my mother had been talking about something they didn't wish me to overhear. There was a tension in both women that was unusual.

I'd always thought the Maharani was beautiful. Slim and attractive, her dark eyes lined with kohl to make them even more exotic, she wore silks woven with gold and silver threads, and the ends of her saris were almost stiff with heavy, shimmering embroidery. The pearls she wore were legendary—long ropes that must weigh on her neck, and the most perfect I'd ever seen in size and quality. On her fingers were huge stones set in gold. Burmese rubies caught the light, along with first water diamonds, sapphires, and even a large square-cut emerald. But she wasn't at all stuffy. She sat in my mother's parlor as comfortably as if she were on the silk and jewel-encrusted cushions in a room three times this size.

As I took my place beside her, I realized she'd dismissed her servants—they were probably having their own tea in my mother's sitting room—and that was another sign that the two women had been holding a very private conversation.

My father came in soon afterward. Tall and handsome in his uniform, he bent over the Maharani's hand and kissed her fingertips. She laughed up at him, and patted the seat on the other side of her. "Come and tell me what you have been doing."

My father, a major at this stage in his career, entertained her with humorous stories, and she laughed and clapped her hands in delight.

"Richard, you make soldiering seem so amusing. And all the while I know you are lying to me in the politest possible way."

He laughed as well, and then with a glance toward me, sitting quietly as I turned the pages of the new book she'd brought me, gave her his view of what was happening politically. None of us ever forgot the dreadful Sepoy Mutiny of 1857, even though it was decades in the past. We never took our safety or the loyalty of the men who served in the army or worked in our houses for granted. I'd been trained from childhood to obey instantly if there was the least sign of trouble. The irrefutable fact was, the British were outnumbered thousands to one, and we could as easily be murdered in our beds as not, if anything went wrong.

It was one of the many reasons parents sent their children to England and safety, to be educated and brought up far away from India. My parents, wiser than most, had kept me with them.

The Maharani listened intently to what he was saying, and then suggested that my father might like to accompany her on a walk in the gardens to see the roses. My mother understood that this wasn't an idle flirtation—it was their only chance to speak freely without being overheard.

When my father had escorted her through the double doors giving onto the verandah, my mother said to me in a low voice, "It's as well you know, my dear. That cousin of the Maharajah's has been causing a great deal of trouble again over some of the reforms being put into place. His Highness has sent his wife to visit us as an opportunity to tell Richard what's happening. He'll know how best to advise Colonel Haldane and consider what we can do to help."

"Will they be all right?" I asked anxiously. For I was very fond of the Maharani and I liked her husband as well. He'd been educated in Britain, and his friends there had called him Harry. His son, my age, and his daughter, a year or so older, had been my playmates since I was in leading strings.

"I'm sure they'll be fine," my mother told me, but there was a tiny echo of doubt in her voice.

I said, "Is there anything that Father can do? Or the colonel? To support the Maharajah?" But that I knew could be a double-edged sword, giving his enemies cause to claim he lived in the pocket of the British. It had been difficult, persuading many of the Indian princes to give up their feudal power for the greater good, relinquishing so much authority to the British Crown. The Maharajah's son, like his father, was to be educated at Eton, leaving in August with his entourage. All of a sudden it dawned on me that possibly he was being sent to where he would be safe.

"I daresay there will be something." Again that tiny echo of doubt in her voice.

At that moment, my father returned with the Maharani, and they smiled as they came through the door. But I'd seen, as they stepped onto the wide verandah, that they hadn't been smiling then.

The Maharani took her leave soon after. She often invited me to come and stay, but this time there was no mention of it.

We followed the Maharani and her entourage out to where her motorcar waited. I remembered that the first time I'd seen her, I was sadly disappointed that she hadn't arrived on an elephant. Now, as my father was handing her into the rear of the motorcar, I looked at her guard, always handsomely dressed, plumes in their caps, sitting astride lovely black horses. Behind them was an assortment of grooms, and as her driver set out for the compound gates, I realized that I'd seen one of those grooms before. It was in the village not an hour ago, and he'd been standing behind one of the stalls near the fortune-teller's tent, talking to a man with a long scar on his face. But what could he possibly have been doing there?

I touched my father's arm. "That groom—I'm sure I saw him today in the village. But he wasn't wearing the Maharani's livery at the time."

My father turned quickly. "Tell me."

If I explained what I'd seen, it would mean confessing to my own escapade. But I could hear the fortune-teller's voice again: *The life of someone you care for is in grave danger. My child, you must go now. Before it is too late.*

Had she been telling my fortune at that point? Or warning me? Had she heard something? Gossip flew about the marketplace like birds on the wing.

Had it been said in an entirely different tone of voice, not the singsong of a pretend trance?

"The village fortune-teller. I think she knew something. It was after Simon had come into the tent, you see. Perhaps the warning was meant for him or even for both of us. Please? Ask Simon."

. . . You must go now. Before it is too late.

If I'd lingered at the bazaar, I'd have arrived too late for the Maharani's visit. Go with this man, she must have meant. Now. Before it's too late.

Of course it was known that the Maharani would be calling on my mother. Her entourage would have been seen arriving at the compound. Everyone talked about whatever the Maharajah or his family did. A new parrot, a new motorcar, a new jewel, a new elephant—it didn't matter, the news would spread on the wind.

My father said urgently to me, "I can't go to the colonel with only the information I've collected from my daughter, my batman, and a fortune-teller. What else do you know? You must tell me."

"I don't know anything else—" I began, beginning to worry in earnest now.

From behind us, Simon cleared his throat. I'd forgotten he was there.

"Because of the heat today, your men haven't been out on patrol yet."

My father wheeled. "You're right. Simon, go and tell them to be ready to ride in five minutes. And make certain each man has a rifle and a pistol. With double the usual amount of ammunition for both." To me he said, "Go inside. Tell your mother what is happening."

"But the Maharani," I argued. "I'm worried about her." Something else occurred to me. "She didn't invite me to visit."

"Yes, she was worried. She didn't want you in the middle of whatever might happen in the next ten days. But you're right about one thing. It's happening *now*, not later. Go on, tell your mother. We might not be back for a while."

I turned and, lifting my skirts, ran across the parade ground to our gate. The gatekeeper tried to stop me, but I broke away. Then I realized what he was saying.

"Little memsahib, wait."

I came to a skidding stop. I could hear my governess calling from the verandah, "Elizabeth! Decorum."

Ignoring her, I said to the porter, "What is it?"

"Three of the men in the Maharani's escort are new. And two of the grooms were armed. I found it strange. Should I tell the Major Sahib?"

In their brilliant uniforms and turban caps, her escort looked so much alike I'd often thought to myself they must be brothers. It was Simon who told me that they were all from the same area where the Maharani had been brought up. Her own loyal people. But what about the new men?

"Was one of the new escorts a man with a scar?" I hadn't noticed him on one of the dark horses, but our gatekeeper would have more time to inspect them as they waited for the Maharani.

"Yes, little memsahib."

I thanked him, turned again and ran as fast as I could toward the lines. I could already hear the jingle of harness, the snorts of the horses, eager for a run, and the voices of the men as they prepared to mount.

Turning the corner beside the stables, I slammed into someone coming fast the other way, nearly knocking the breath out of me.

Hands grasped my shoulders, setting me back on my feet. I looked up. It was Simon.

"What are you doing here? Go on, go back to the house."

I caught his hand. "Simon, listen." I gave him the message from the gatekeeper.

Simon, frowning, said, "Why didn't he tell your father? Or the Maharani's aide-de-camp?"

"I don't know—yes, I do, my father was already on his way to the lines. He didn't come back to the house after the Maharani had left."

"Good girl," Simon told me. "Now go. They won't wait for me."

He raced down to the lines, caught the reins of his horse from one of the sergeants, and swung into the saddle. I watched as the troop formed up on command and headed out into the open country beyond the cantonment. Simon waited until they were wheeling toward the north, where the Maharani had come from, then spurred his mount to where my father rode next to Captain Dixon. Their heads were close for a moment, and then Simon fell back to his place in the ranks.

Relieved, I walked briskly back to the house, and listened to Miss Stewart's scolding with as much repentance as I could muster. When she had finished, ordering me to my room at once, I begged her first to let me give my mother the message from my father.

She relented—she had, I thought, a fondness for my father than she had kept concealed with prim care—and let me go into the parlor, where my mother was looking at the book the Maharani had brought me.

"This is very interesting, Bess," she began, then looked at me more intently. "What is it? What's happened?"

Walking across the room to stand by her chair, I whispered my news, even including my visit to the fortune-teller. Outside on the verandah the men who sat cross-legged and kept the fans moving above our heads in the heat were singing softly to themselves, but I took no chances at being overheard.

My mother listened carefully. "Well done, Bess," she said, when I'd finished. "But Simon's right, you mustn't go into the bazaar alone. It isn't wise."

"But how did the fortune-teller know something was wrong?" I asked. "I refuse to believe she could see into the future."

"She could have overheard something." She sat there, the book closed on her finger to hold her place, her gaze thoughtful. "Fortune-tellers must know a variety of dialects, otherwise they couldn't ply their trade all across the country. Someone who thought he was speaking confidentially might have been within hearing of her tent."

Miss Stewart tapped politely at the door, then came into the room. "You've spoken to your mother, Elizabeth. Now to your room."

With a sigh, I took my punishment without complaint, but I sat at the windows of my room, longing to be riding with my father and Simon and the men in his command. What was happening? Had they caught up to the entourage? This had been a private visit, not an official one. The Maharani had come with only a small escort. Perhaps, I thought, so as not to raise suspicion?

What was the point of the warning? Was she to be killed? Or captured and held to make her husband do as he was told? He loved his wife, it had been more than an arranged marriage. Would he agree to her kidnappers' demands? Yes, surely he would, if that would save her from death or torture or mutilation. I shivered at the thought. But the cousin who was giving the Maharajah so much trouble was a wild sort, the son of the Maharajah's father's favorite concubine, spoiled and always ungrateful for his education and position. Until the Maharajah's son had been born, this cousin had touted himself as the heir to the throne, much to the annoyance of the state and the British government. And then I remembered a story I'd heard when first we came to this province. The Maharajah's only brother, the only man who stood between the Maharajah and this cousin, had been trampled by an elephant gone rogue. Or had it? That had been shortly after the Maharajah had taken a wife. There were several versions of what had happened. Of course elephants did sometimes turn rogue. It was why ceremonial elephants were usually female. But they could be goaded into action as well.

I couldn't sit there, simply waiting. I slipped out my window, hurried through the garden—avoiding the gate, where I'd be seen—and sat down on a tree trunk by the wall that surrounded our compound. A breeze touched my face, lifting tendrils of hair, blessedly cool. And somewhere in the distance I heard a rumble of thunder.

Or was it gunfire?

I moved into the open, scanning the sky. This was the hot season, not the rainy season. There wasn't a cloud to be seen in any direction.

Gunfire then. It must be. And it went on for several minutes before the volleys grew more ragged.

My heart was in my throat. My father—Simon—men in the ranks I'd known for years—they were all out there, in danger. I strained to listen.

It seemed to be coming nearer. Had the troublemakers been routed? But why were they coming back this way? To hide in the village until they could manage to escape? It didn't make any sense. Who would protect them?

I could hear horses now, coming fast.

I sat there, straining my ears to listen. I almost missed the flash of color on the far side of the garden. There it was again, and all at once I heard Miss Stewart scream. It came from the summerhouse, the little wicker house where we sometimes sat in the cool of the evening. Miss Stewart often went there to read.

I was on my feet and running before it dawned on me that to go to her rescue would mean putting myself in danger, and as the daughter of an officer, I was a far more important hostage than a governess. People were shouting now, the men who pulled the fans, the kitchen staff, the porter at the gate. I could hear my mother's voice, and then she broke off in mid-word.

Had she been taken as well?

I ran for the low wall that surrounded our quarters, climbed over that into the next garden, which belonged to Captain Dixon and his wife, and raced toward the barracks. I burst through the door of the first one I came to. There were half a hundred men there, some of them just coming off duty, others getting ready to take their turn, and a handful sleeping or playing cards. At sight of me, a dozen men sprang to their feet, staring. Some of them were out of uniform, and a sergeant stepped forward at once, blocking my view, saying, "*Miss Crawford*—" in reprimand.

"Sergeant Barton," I said, fighting for breath, "something's wrong at our bungalow. There's been a skirmish—the patrol. I think one of the men they're chasing has come back to the house. They've got Miss Stewart, and possibly my mother—"

They hadn't waited to hear me out. Sergeant Barton was saying grimly, "I told you it was gunfire, not rifle practice," as he set me aside and hurried out the door.

I followed, in amongst the men who'd caught up their rifles. "Please, be careful of my mother—Miss Stewart—"

But they had already turned toward the gardens of the Dixon bungalow, next to ours, brushing past the porter at the gate. I saw the old man's anxious face, and knew he must have heard the cries from my house.

We cut across the garden, and the men leapt over the low wall, bending low, using the trees and shrubs for protection as they made their way to this side of our bungalow. I could see the kitchen quarters now, the servants standing stock—still, looking toward the far side of the house, as quiet as if they'd been struck dumb.

I caught up with Sergeant Barton as he reached the side of the house and turned to deploy his men. "My window—" I pointed to it. He turned to see that it was open, in spite of the heat. Nodding, he motioned to two of his men, then to the window.

"They don't know their way. I do," I said quickly. "I can show them how to reach the other side of the house. They can see the summerhouse from my father's study. I think that's where whoever it is found Miss Stewart."

He stared at me for a moment, then nodded again. This time he boosted me up and back through the window.

Just then I heard the patrol coming into the horse lines. Leaning out, I whispered, "My father—he's back. Someone must warn him, or he may be walking into an ambush."

The sergeant turned to order one of his men to the horse lines, and I took the opportunity to walk quietly across my room to the closed door. I listened carefully, but didn't hear anyone. Two privates, cursing under their breath, were following me into my room. I put my finger to my lips, and gently, slowly, opened the door into the passage.

All was quiet. Too quiet. I gestured for the two men to follow me, and I crept as silently as I could down the passage to my father's study. That door stood open—he hadn't come back to shut it after seeing the Maharani off. I ducked low, so that I couldn't be seen by anyone watching the study windows. When I could do it safely, I got to my feet and carefully peered around the curtains.

I could see the summerhouse, just as I knew I could. Miss Stewart was standing in the doorway, and even from here I could see that she was trembling. In the shadows behind her, there was only darkness. And then I saw movement, and the glint of light on what was surely a revolver. Whoever he was, he was kneeling just behind her, hidden from view by her skirts.

But where was my mother?

The two men had caught up with me, and I told them in a whisper what I'd seen.

"She's simply standing there, a decoy. With someone holding a revolver behind her. I don't see my mother. I don't know where she is."

And then I could hear Miss Stewart's voice. It was hardly recognizable, quavering, high pitched, clearly badly frightened. "Mrs. Crawford? Please—please come out. He'll shoot me if you don't. Please?"

My mother wasn't there! I breathed a sigh of relief. But what to do to save Miss Stewart?

The sergeant had crept up behind us in the study, and I was sure he'd heard her plea.

"Where do you think your mother is?" he asked me in a hoarse whisper.

"In her parlor. It's where I left her a little while ago."

"Go to her. Carefully, now! Ask her to keep them occupied in the summerhouse while some of my men try to circle it."

I nodded, then made my way out of the study. Creeping down the passage again, I saw that the parlor door was also standing open. Dropping to my knees, I crawled to it and into the room.

Someone near the window whirled, and I saw the muzzle of a revolver pointed straight at me before my mother realized who was there and lowered it.

"Bess!" The word was little more than a hiss.

I crawled over to her, and she held my hand as I told her what the sergeant had said. "But you can't go out there, or he'll have two hostages. And that's worse."

Mother nodded, then it was her turn to put her finger to her lips, just as Miss Stewart called again.

Mother raised her voice. "I'm afraid. I'm too afraid," she cried, and it was strange to hear a woman holding a revolver pleading fear.

"Please, you must," Miss Stewart begged.

"Where's my daughter? I want to know where she is—if she's safe. I won't come out until I know she's all right." Her voice was quavering nearly as badly as Miss Stewart's, but my mother's eyes were angry, her face set.

"I—I don't know where she is," Miss Stewart said. "I sent her to her room."

"She's not there. Don't lie to me. I won't move from here. Her room is empty, I tell you!"

"Please, don't worry about her, Mrs. Crawford. Come out, now, or he'll kill me."

I crawled away, back to the study. There was still one soldier there, watching events in the summerhouse. He motioned for me to be careful, and after a moment I joined him at the window. Looking out, I thought my governess was on the verge of collapse. Her face was pale, her hands shaking as she held them down against her skirts.

"I can't trust you, if you won't tell me where my child is," Mother was saying.

A hand on my shoulder nearly made me leap out of my skin.

It was Simon, and he was breathing hard, as if he'd been running.

"Tell me what's happening."

I gave him a very brief account. He nodded. "Stay here. Count to ten, and then start crying for your mother."

I wanted to argue, but he was gone, slipping like a shadow out of the room. But where was my father? If Simon was here, he wouldn't be very far away.

I counted to ten, then raised my voice and began to cry. "I'm here, Mother, I'm here, what's happened to Miss Stewart? Where's my father? What's happening?"

Just then another voice crossed over mine. It came from the far corner of the verandah, I was sure of it.

"Major Crawford here," it said, but it wasn't my father speaking. It was Simon, although he sounded very much like my father. "I'm unarmed. Let her go and I'll come out."

I could see Miss Stewart's head turn as if she were listening to instructions from whomever it was holding her hostage.

"You must come out first," she said then. "He won't let me go until he sees you're unarmed."

Very clever, I thought. We now knew there was only one man in that summerhouse.

My mother's voice, seemingly filled with fright, called, "Richard? Please, don't do it. Don't step out. He'll kill you, and Miss Stewart as well."

Simon, still speaking as if he were my father, said, "Can't you see that poor woman is about to faint? Let her go, and I'll do anything you ask."

Almost in that same instant, Miss Stewart went down in what appeared to be a dead faint, and Simon must have stepped out into the open. Out of the corner of my eye, I saw him standing there, unarmed just as he'd said. My heart turned over, and I heard my mother gasp.

I saw the man in the summerhouse rise to his feet, leveling his revolver. But before he could fire a single shot, another one rang out and the man went down.

Simon went bounding into the summerhouse, bending over, reaching out for something. Then I saw him pocket a revolver. He turned to Miss Stewart, but she was already sitting up, a weak smile on her face. My father came sliding down from the banyan tree near the wall. I saw his boots before the rest of him appeared, and his revolver was still in his hand. Using Simon as a decoy to give him time to get into position, my father, had had a clear view of the man holding Miss Stewart at gunpoint. As soon as she had fallen down in a faint, my father has also had a clean shot. Between them and he and Simon had come up with a hasty but clever plan.

He quickly joined Simon at the summerhouse, and together they reached in and pulled out a man in the livery of the Maharani's grooms. He was shot through the shoulder, his right arm hanging limp down by his side, but his face was twisted in fury. I saw him spit in Simon's direction, but Simon had already leapt back.

My father, quite angry, helped Miss Stewart to her feet.

I went racing to the parlour, where my mother was leaning against the wall, the revolver still clutched in her hand. Her face was pale.

"I was so afraid he'd hurt her before I could get a clear shot. Thank God your father came in time," she said, then smiled at me. "Are you all right, love?" she asked me, straightening up to put her arm around me.

I could see, through the window, that Miss Stewart was clinging to Simon as if to a lifeline, and my father was just handing the wounded man over to Sergeant Barton.

As the man turned toward the house, I could see for the first time that he was the one with the ugly scar across his face. And then Sergeant Barton and a corporal were leading him away, out of the garden toward the colonel's office.

My father looked up at the house, and came striding toward the verandah and the parlour door. He came through it like a whirlwind, scooping my mother into his arms and holding her close. Over her head, he grimaced at me.

"And just how many more rules have you broken this day?" he said to me. "Bursting into the barracks without permission, leading a foray into the garden and crawling through your own window, not to mention invading my study with armed men."

Ignoring that, I said quickly, "The Maharani—is she all right? And the rest of these men who wanted to harm her? What's become of them?"

"Your father managed to do a bit of the work himself, you know," he said, the grimace fading into a grin. "We got there in time, although those men put up quite a fight. But it was short lived. The one with the scar got away, and we tried to catch him before he reached the compound. But we were delayed by the mopping up. The Maharani is well, and she sends her love."

My mother moved away from his embrace. "I was so worried for you," she said, touching his face before adding, "I must see to Miss Stewart. A cup of hot tea, I think, with a little of your brandy in it, if you don't mind, my dear."

She handed him the revolver and strode out of the parlor toward the garden. I watched her reach out to help Simon with the still-shaken governess.

My father's face was stern when he turned to me. "You took too many unnecessary risks," he said.

"It was Mother who was at risk. I was on the other side of the garden when it started."

"It could have been you and not Miss Stewart in his clutches."

"That's true," I admitted, knowing he was right. "What were they going to do? Take the Maharani as hostage? Or kill her?"

"It appears that they were expecting to force the Maharajah to give up his title in favor of his cousin, and then leave for exile in England." My father looked toward the garden and the summerhouse. "I'd wager he and the Maharani wouldn't have made it to Bombay alive, even if he'd agreed to leave."

"What will happen to the cousin now?"

"I shan't inquire too closely," my father said. "I was told once that there was an old dungeon beneath the palace. It hasn't been used in two generations. I shouldn't be surprised if it's occupied for a while."

I could hear Colonel Haldane's voice on the path leading up to our door. My father heard it too.

"Least in sight," he said to me, then put his arms around me for a brief moment before hurrying to intercept his commanding officer.

I went out into the passage toward my room, as I'd been ordered—but I went out the window again to look for Simon. I wanted a full account of everything that had happened. I knew my father wouldn't tell me any more than he had, but I could cajole Simon into describing the action.

I spotted him leaving the garden by a roundabout way so that he wouldn't encounter Colonel Haldane, and as I hurried to catch him up, it occurred to me that if I hadn't gone to the fortune-teller, the Maharani might well be in very real difficulty now. But it was Simon who had remembered that the patrol hadn't been out today, giving my father the excuse he needed to act quickly, without consulting the colonel. My father ought to promote Simon for that, even if it meant losing him as his batman.

Busy with my thoughts, I was halfway across the garden before I realized that I hadn't done my duty. I stopped, hesitated, and then turned back to the house. The exciting details of the skirmish would have to wait. I needed to find my mother and Miss Stewart, to be sure my governess was all right. She was the one who'd suffered most at the hands of the man with the scarred face. And she must still be anxious, even though the worst was over. I didn't know if she'd actually fainted, or if she'd been clever enough to pretend to. It didn't matter. She had been terribly brave at a very bad time.

As I clambered back through my window again and started toward the passage door and Miss Stewart's room, one down from mine, I sighed.

I'd had a far more exciting afternoon than merely going to the village fortune-teller. But I'd been my father's daughter long enough to know I couldn't possibly write to my friends in England and tell them all about it. What had happened would be hushed up, for the Government's ears only. And to protect the Maharajah.

I tapped on Miss Stewart's door, then stepped into the room. She was lying on the bed, a cool cloth on her forehead, and some color had returned to her face. She was thanking my mother for saving her life. She turned to smile at me.

"It's a good thing I sent you to your room," she said. "You might have been in the summerhouse with me, doing your lessons. I just hope you weren't too frightened, hearing what that man made me say to your mother."

I glanced up at my mother, then smiled in return. "No, Miss Stewart. I knew my father wouldn't let anything happen to you or her."

"There's my brave girl," Miss Stewart said approvingly.

Over her head, my mother, quite relieved, nodded to me.

Very likely nothing more would be said about my foray into the bazaar to find the fortune-teller. My father, Simon, and Sergeant Barton could be counted on not to speak about the rest of the afternoon.

But a week later a silk-wrapped packet addressed to me arrived at our door, brought by a liveried messenger from the Maharani.

In the packet was a velvet case holding the loveliest rope of pearls, as fine as any I'd ever seen her wear. There was no message in the case, although I did look.

My mother let me admire them for a time, then closed the case. "When you are older," she said. "It would attract too much attention for you to be seen to wear them at your age."

It didn't matter. I understood. And I could guess too why they'd been sent without a note. My father had told the Maharani, if no one else, what had really transpired that day. I knew he trusted her not to speak of it. I was glad she knew, because I cared about her.

Nothing was said about those events when next she came to call on my mother. It was as if nothing had happened since her last visit. Nor did she ask why I wasn't wearing her pearls.

Read on for a sneak peek at the latest

Bess Crawford mystery

A PATTERN OF LIES

On sale August 18, 2015

Chapter One

Canterbury, Kent, Autumn 1918

I DIDN'T KNOW much about the little town of Cranbourne, on The Swale in northeastern Kent, only that its abbey had been destroyed by a very angry Henry VIII when the abbot of the day refused to take the King's side in certain matters. What stone was left had been transported to France to shore up the English-owned harbor in Calais. A young Lieutenant by the name of Merrill, standing by me at the railing of the *Sea Maid,* had told me about that as we came through the roads and edged toward where we were to dock. That was in 1915. Shortly after that, we were caught up in the rush of disembarking and finding our respective transports, and I doubt I gave it another thought.

My next encounter with Cranbourne was while I was assigned to a base hospital in France. A critically ill patient was brought in for further surgery, and he sometimes talked about the village during his long and painful recovery.

All in the past, that.

And then yesterday I accompanied a convoy of badly wounded men to hospital in a village just outside Canterbury, in Kent. The hospital specialized in internal wounds, and it was a shorter journey to go directly there than to travel all the way to London first, and then arrange transport all the way back.

They'd made the crossing from France safely, every one of my patients, even though Matron had been worried about the gravest cases. All the same, I was relieved to find a line of ambulances waiting for us in Dover, and again when the train pulled into Canterbury's railway station. Soon after that we had every man in a cot with a minimum of fuss. Most of them were too exhausted to speak, but they knew they were in England, and their smiles were enough. Home. Alive. And on the way to recovery. I hoped it was true. Then I saw Lieutenant Harriman, the most seriously wounded, weakly giving me a thumbs-up, and I thought, *Yes, they'll be all right now!*

By three in the morning, we'd coaxed them to swallow a little thin broth before wearily seeking our own beds, leaving the night staff in charge at last.

Late the next morning, I said good-bye to the men and to the nurses who had come over with me. They were needed in France, but I had earned a few days of leave.

One of the doctors kindly ran me back into Canterbury to await my train to London.

I was happily counting the minutes before I could call my parents in Somerset and tell them when to expect me in Victoria Station when I discovered that my train was delayed. Three *hours*, the stationmaster informed me, although from his gloomy expression, I didn't hold out much hope of reaching London until midnight at the earliest. *Well, so much for that*, I thought, resigned to further delays. My telephone call would have to wait until I knew more.

Rather than sit in the busy, noisy railway station, I decided to walk for a bit. It was a fine day, and I'd always enjoyed Canterbury. Leaving my kit bag in the growing pile of luggage pushed to one side for the London train, I looked at my watch to check the time, then set out.

A handsome town with its bustling markets and its famous cathedral, the one always associated with the tomb of the Black Prince and the martyrdom of Thomas à Becket, Canterbury had much to offer. I could pass a pleasant hour or two exploring, and then call in again at the station for the latest news. If the train was still delayed, I could count on a quiet lunch somewhere nearby, and even browse in the shops, although many of them had very little to offer these days.

Before very long, I came across a hidden gem of a garden open to strollers. Half an hour spent enjoying the autumn flowers blooming along a narrow stream was heavenly. There was so little left of beauty in the parts of France I saw every

day, only the hardy poppies and a few wildflowers that strag-
gled in any patch of rough ground. I badly needed something
else to think about besides torn bodies and bloody bandages,
consoling amputees and long vigils at the sides of dying men.
Sitting on one of the benches, I closed my eyes and listened to
the bees in the blossoms at my feet. For once I couldn't hear
the guns in France, and I let the Front fade away.

Over my head in one of the lovely old trees growing along
the stream, a jackdaw began to call, confused by this sudden
burst of warm weather here in the autumn. I smiled as I listened to him.

Feeling myself again, I set out for the High Street shops.
Along the way I passed the Army recruiting office where men
could enlist. In the early days of the war, August and Septem-
ber 1914, in particular, these had been nearly overwhelmed
with volunteers, men who were determined to get into the
fight before the Kaiser changed his mind and sued for peace.
It didn't quite happen that way, and it wasn't long before the
Government had had to turn to conscription to fill the ranks.

The office looked rather forlorn, and through the open
door, where a shaft of warm sunlight lit up the posters and
the enlistment forms and the polished shoes of the officer
seated behind the desk, I could almost catch a feeling of res-
ignation. As if, with the war ending, this little room, once
a small shop, had lost its usefulness and was just waiting
for someone in London to remember it existed and close it

down. A sign, perhaps, that the war *would* end, that no more men would be asked to die for King and Country.

Strolling with no particular goal in mind, I soon found myself making my way toward the cathedral precincts. This was a lovely place to spend a quiet hour, and when I came to the massive Christ Church Gate set into the high wall, I stepped through it and walked down to where I had the best view of the west front.

For a moment I simply stood there, looking up at the three ornate towers. It occurred to me how fortunate the French had been not to lose any of their great cathedrals. Damaged, some of them, but they would survive. Far too many of their lovely old village churches had fallen to artillery barrages. The sun was warm on my face, the view splendid, and in spite of the others here in the broad precincts, passing me on the walk, I was reluctant to step inside just yet.

Someone called my name.

"Bess? Sister Crawford? Is that you?"

I turned toward the speaker, and he exclaimed, "Good Lord, it is!"

I didn't recognize him at first.

He had filled out, his dark hair thick now and well cut. It had been shaved to attend to his head wound, although it was the wound in his side that we thought would surely kill him. But it didn't, although he'd been quite thin and gaunt by the time he'd been stable enough to transport to England.

"Captain Ashton," I exclaimed, and held out my hand in greeting as he came to meet me. But he grasped the hand and leaned forward to kiss me on the cheek. "How *well* you look."

"Thanks to you and the good doctors. And it's Major now," he added, touching his insignia. "How are you? And what are you doing in Canterbury?"

I explained about the wounded, and he nodded. "It's a good hospital. I spent some weeks there myself, if you remember. Do you have time for a cup of tea?"

"Yes, in fact, I do," I said. "They've no idea when my train will come in, and I've been passing the morning seeing the sights. Two minutes more and I'd have been inside the cathedral, admiring the stained glass windows."

"My luck that you hadn't gone inside. Otherwise, I'd have missed you." He fell in step beside me, offering his arm. There was the slightest sign of a limp in his gait, but he walked steadily along the path, and I was glad to see it.

Captain Ashton—as he was then—had been very popular with the nursing staff. He was an attractive man, of course, but his sense of humor in the face of his severe wounds had won our admiration. Refusing the morphine as often as he could manage it, he did everything he was told with a smile, however shaky that smile might be, and made light of his suffering. It was true, there were many in that surgical ward in far worse shape than he was, but we'd worried endlessly that we might finally lose him to infection and loss of blood.

"I don't have to ask how you are, Bess," he was saying. "You look well. Tired, yes, God knows, don't we all? But still the prettiest Sister in the ward."

I looked up at him. "And you haven't lost your skill at flattery. I thought you were to be married as soon as you'd recovered?"

As I watched, a shadow crossed his face. "Yes, well. She died. In the first wave of the Spanish flu. I didn't get home in time. They were burying her when I arrived."

"I am so very sorry, Major." I meant it. I'd read him letters from his betrothed when he was too ill to read them himself, and written to her as well, to answer for him. Eloise was her name, though he called her Ellie, and I'd come to know her, in a way. I couldn't think of a finer match for this man. I had so wanted him to survive and come back to her. A small victory for two people amidst the chaos of war.

"I wouldn't have had her suffer another hour. But I could have wished she'd lived until I was there to hold her hand." He looked up at the tall cathedral gates to hide his pain. "But there it is." Clearing his throat, he said, as he had so many times in the ward, "This too shall pass us by."

We walked on in silence, and just beyond the gates he found a tearoom and ordered for both of us.

For a time we chatted companionably. About mutual friends, about those we'd lost, about the prospects, finally, of peace. I asked about his parents, and he asked after my mother and the Colonel Sahib.

"What brings you to Canterbury? Are you on leave, or on your way back to France?"

His fingers toyed with the milk jug for a moment, and then he said, "I've had trouble with my hearing. It's coming back now, but when the tunnel went up nearly beneath our feet, I wouldn't have heard an artillery barrage. I was luckier than some of the lads. The shock wave killed them. At any rate, I was sent home and told to give it time. I don't think the doctors in France held out much hope, but I've got another week before I meet with the medical board, and I have every reason to think they'll clear me now. Of course, if they whisper all their questions, I might still be in trouble," he ended with a smile.

Laughing, I said, "That's wonderful news. Still, I'm sure your mother was glad to have you safe with her for a little while."

"Look, why not come home with me for an hour or two? My mother will be very happy to see you."

"Do you live here in Canterbury now?" I asked.

"No. But not all that far from here. Not by motorcar. Cranbourne. It's a small village up on The Swale."

"Cranbourne," I repeated, all at once remembering. "Of course. And it had an abbey in the distant past."

"A ruined abbey," he said, nodding. "Did I tell you about it? I must have done." Without waiting for an answer, he went on. "I ran in this morning to speak to the police. But Inspector Brothers isn't in. I was told to come back later."

"The police?" I asked, surprised.

He looked out the tearoom window, not meeting my eyes. "There's been a spot of trouble. The police seem to be dragging their feet doing anything about it. Nothing to worry you about. But it would cheer my mother to no end to see you again."

When the Major—then Captain Ashton—had been so severely wounded, somehow Mrs. Ashton had got permission to come over to France and nurse her son. A small woman with snow-white hair, the same lovely blue eyes as the Major, and a spine of steel, she refused utterly to believe that he would die, and without getting in the way of the nursing staff, she sat beside him and read to him and fed him broth without a single tear shed. Only one evening, I'd discovered her in a room where we stored supplies, her face buried in a towel so that no one would hear her. It was the only time. I never knew where she went to cry after that. Or if there had only been that one moment of weakness.

"How lovely," I said, and meant it. "But first I should be sure about my train. There might be news."

"We'll call in at the railway station first."

"Then I'd like to go, very much."

"Good." He settled our bill and guided me down the street to where he'd left his motorcar.

News of my train was not very reassuring.

"There's a troop train coming through shortly, and it will be filled with wounded going back," the harassed stationmaster told us. "I'd find a room, if I were you, Sister. It could be morning before I've got anything for you."

"Never mind," the Major said. "But let's collect your kit, shall we?"

I looked at the baggage—now piled high by the side of the station, even overflowing onto the platform. I could just see mine squeezed between a large steamer trunk and the wall.

"A very good idea," I agreed, and Major Ashton helped me extract it. I could just picture what my clean uniforms must look like now, crumpled into a wrinkled twist. But there would be an iron I could borrow in Mrs. Ashton's kitchen.

As we walked back to his motorcar, he said, "There's more than enough room at the Hall. The hotels are crowded, and you'll be better off with us."

I protested that I didn't intend to presume on his mother's hospitality, but he said firmly, "Nonsense. You can't wander around this town all day, only to discover there will be no train after all. Tomorrow the lines should be straightened out."

I hoped he was right. I still had my heart set on reaching London.

And so we threaded our way out of Canterbury and took the main road toward Rochester, the old Watling Street of the Romans.

The countryside was so beautiful. Roadside wildflowers had gone to seed, but the hedgerows were still thick and green, and sometimes trees along the way provided a canopy of cool shadows overhead.

Major Ashton said, his eyes on the road, "Do you think you could manage to call me Mark? God knows we've known each other for several years. It wouldn't be improper, would it? And 'Sister Crawford' reminds me too much of my wounds."

We were not encouraged to call patients by their first names. It fostered a familiarity that was unprofessional. But the Major was no longer my patient, and so I said, "Thank you. Mark, then."

"Much better." He turned his head and grinned at me. Those blue eyes were twinkling. "I still look over my shoulder when someone calls 'Major' to see who it is they're speaking to."

He was young to have achieved his majority. Thirty? But the war had seen the deaths of so many officers that it was more a mark of survival than time served, as it had been before the war.

We were enjoying the drive in silence when the Major said, "Bess, don't say anything about the explosion."

"When the tunnel went up?" I asked, turning to him in surprise. "Doesn't your family know that's how you lost your hearing?"

It was his turn to be surprised. "Sorry. No. The explosion and fire in Cranbourne. Hadn't you heard about it? Two years ago, it was. I wasn't here, but it must have been as bad as anything in France. Over a hundred men were killed."

"I didn't know—what happened?" I couldn't imagine anything in a village that could cause such terrible damage.

"It was the gunpowder mill. No one knows what happened. It just—blew up."

I remembered then that his family owned a mill where gunpowder had been made for over a century, and in early 1915, the Government stepped in and took it over, increasing size and production to meet the needs of a nation at war.

"There was a fire as well," he was saying. "God knows whether it was the cause of the main explosion or if it started afterward in the dust. I can't believe anyone survived the blast. Still, no one could get to them in time, and that has haunted my father to this day. It was a Sunday, Bess. There were no women in the mill because it was Sunday. Or the loss of life would have been unthinkable."

"How awful!"

He took a deep breath. "Everyone's first thought was sabotage. Well, the mill is close by The Swale, it could have happened that way. A small boat putting in at night? Easier to believe that than think the unthinkable, that it was caused by carelessness. At any rate, the Government sent half a hundred men down here, scrambling over the ruins almost before they had cooled. They searched the marshes for any sign of a boat sent in by a submarine or even a small ship out in the Thames roads; they searched houses and barns and woods and even the abbey ruins in the event the Germans had sent a party in force and it was still hiding somewhere. For six months we had German fever. The captain who was our liaison with the Army was insistent that it must be sabotage, and so neighbor looked at neighbor, wondering who might be a secret German sympathizer. My father was very worried, I can tell you, with suspicion rampant, and even his own movements looked into. Unbelievably ugly. And then the Government found no evidence to support that theory and simply went away."

The amount of gunpowder produced here must have been of immense value to the war effort. The Germans would have been delighted to see the mill put out of business. There had already been a gunpowder crisis that had shaken even the Government. And of course a mill *had* to be located near water, because water was needed in the manufacture as well as to transport the gunpowder to the scattered factories where shell and cartridge casings would be filled with it. No one wanted to see wagons of gunpowder on the rutted and wretched roads.

"And then?"

"It was assumed that something must have gone wrong, that a spark must have set off the chain reaction. It's a dangerous business to start with, milling the ingredients and producing something that can be used in shells and ammunition. The powder has to go off, of course, when fired. But God help us, not before. Everyone knew it meant hazardous working conditions. It's why the pay was so good. But some felt the Government had been pushing too hard to increase production, ignoring proper safety precautions. My father was often at odds with Captain Collier over that. Still, the demand was there. All of us knew it. The Army alone, never mind the Navy, could have used twice the powder we produced."

He said nothing for a moment. And watching his hands clench on the wheel, I knew there was worse to come.

"Recently, don't ask me why, there have been different whispers. New rumors. Gossip. Finger pointing. It began with more questions about the fire. How that had started— when—and why it had been so intense. Whether it had been deliberately set."

"Deliberately—but that's tantamount to *murder*."

"Precisely. It makes no sense at all. Still, it was well known that my father had never been happy with the Government's terms when they took over, and it was whispered that he was afraid, given the improvements they'd made, that they would refuse to turn the mill over to him again when the war ended."

"Your father?" I repeated. I had never met him, but I did know Mark, and I knew Mrs. Ashton. I couldn't imagine either of them putting money before the lives of the people who had worked for them before the war, even though those same people might be employed by the War Office or the Army for the duration. It was impossible to imagine.

"Mark, perhaps you should take me back to Canterbury. I can't believe your parents will want visitors in the midst of such worries." He'd meant well, but now I could see it was not the best of ideas. "They have enough on their minds."

"On the contrary. You aren't *someone,* a casual acquaintance. You saved my life. You'll be good for their spirits. Look. I didn't intend to tell you any of this, Bess, but I thought, if you'd read about the explosion, you might say something, a sympathetic comment acknowledging what my father must have been through. At any rate, it's my mother I'm most worried about. She tries to keep our spirits up, but I know she's afraid for my father if this wild suspicion gets out of hand. I can't believe it's likely to go too far, but then it's my father we're talking about, and she's vulnerable."

"What does your father have to say about the accusations?"

"Very little. He tends to think that anyone who knows him will recognize them as the foolishness they are." Mark glanced across at me. "My father has always been a proud man. He tries to live up to his duties and obligations and expects other people to measure him by how well he succeeds. Some find that—I think the word would probably be *distant,* or *impersonal.* But he's been responsible for the livelihood of a good many families, and he takes that seriously. I don't think any of those trying to bring him down understands how much the destruction of the mill has affected him. They couldn't believe what they do, if they knew."

We'd been angling north and a little west, and I could hear seagulls in the distance. Out there somewhere to my right would be the Thames Estuary, broad and emptying into the Channel.

"But surely he can tell them where he was, when it happened."

"That's just it. He was seen earlier talking to someone just outside the mill. And then when the explosions began, first the large one and then the smaller ones that followed, he was on his way home. He ran back down to the River Cran. It was low tide, so he waded across, and started toward the mill just as the dust was settling. He stopped and just stood there, looking at the wreckage, shaking his head. Others had run toward the blast as well, and they saw him. For some reason, he just turned and started back the way he'd come. He told me later he was going after men and whatever tools he could find, to try to look for survivors. Before he'd even reached that side of the Cran, the first flames were spotted."

I thought to myself, *Oh dear.* For those looking for answers to explain the deaths of their loved ones, there was always enough circumstantial evidence to support whispers and rumors and finger-pointing. Sudden shocking death was unbelievable, unbearable, and people needed someone, human or divine, to blame for their loss.

I said, trying for a lighter note, "Surely those who know your father well will prevail. The fact that he rushed to the scene shows he cared, that he would have helped if he could. If anything at all could have been done for those poor men."

"God, I hope so. I don't want to go back to France leaving my family in such straits. The trouble is, even our friends have begun to fall away. They've made excuses of course, but it's clear they must be having doubts of their own. Or are reluctant to find themselves included in the rumors and gossip. Whatever the reason, they've simply avoided us. My mother's circle of friends has been particularly distant. She pretends it doesn't matter, but I know it must hurt."

We had come down a long hill through the outskirts of the village, mainly Victorian cottages and bungalows, straggling down toward its heart. Soon we were among the shops and a collection of older buildings, a number of which appeared to date to the days when the abbey flourished. Almshouses, lodgings for guests, abbey offices? A few had been converted to other uses, but it appeared that people still lived in many of them. One was particularly charming, with window boxes of geraniums and stone urns beside the ancient wooden door. And then we were in a small but busy square. I couldn't help but notice the glances as we drove through. Followed by a quick turn of the back as people recognized the motorcar. Even I could see that they were deliberately shunning us. A refusal to acknowledge so much as setting eyes on an Ashton—not even curious to see who else was in the vehicle. I felt an uncomfortable chill. In some fashion their snubs seemed worse than hostile stares would have been.

For Mark's sake I tried to keep my eyes on the attractive older houses scattered about the square, giving it its charm. But I was well aware of what he must be feeling.

We followed the street out of the square, and soon I could just pick out the roofs of buildings along the river. Three of the roofs looked fairly new.

"Why did you wish to speak to the Canterbury police?" I asked, reminded by a glimpse of the police station down a side street.

"There have been some—problems. Property damage mostly. The local constable isn't keen on dealing with it. I decided to have a word with Inspector Brothers." He cast a quick smile my way. "I promise you, no one will come crashing through the windows as we sit down to lunch."

I was of two opinions about that. But I could also better understand why he felt a visit from me might take his mother's mind off what was happening. If only for a few hours.

We turned off into another narrower street where I could see the long high wall that must once have enclosed the abbey. As old as it was, the wall was surprisingly intact, with trees on both sides of it and shaded walks following it. A nursemaid with a child in a pram was strolling along there, a brown-and-white dog trotting by her side.

The Major only followed the wall for a short distance, turning away, then turning again, and soon we were running down toward the River Cran. I could now see the sheds by the water, the sort that seem to line quays everywhere, catering to the needs of ships and boats. Some of them were long enough for sail mending or making rope from raw hemp. Beyond, on the far side of the river, the land rose slightly higher than this side, rough ground at a guess.

I expected the Major to continue to the river, but he stopped just above the sheds, where the road began to slope sharply toward the water. And I could see that what I'd thought was rough ground must actually be the ruins of the powder mill.

I noticed that Mark didn't turn off the motor. We weren't getting down, then.

At first I wasn't really certain what I *was* seeing. There was so little left to tell me what had once been here.

On the far side of the little river, tall grass had taken over. Scattered through it were stones that were nearly invisible here at the end of summer's growth. A jumble of them, without definition. About fifty yards farther on was what appeared to be an open wood that had been caught in a very bad storm. A dozen or so trees had struggled to leaf out, but most were torn and shredded and some were even beginning to show signs of rot, limbs dangling, bark peeling. I realized that the mill had been set in the wood, to keep the buildings cool and to lessen the blast force if something went wrong. Only this time the wood too had suffered badly.

Among the trees lay even more rubble from the powder works, and I began, slowly, to pick out the jagged remnants of roofless walls, stumps of foundations, clusters of unidentifiable stones that could have been anything. There were even what appeared to be corners that no longer had sides. It was as if a fretful child had begun to build a village, tired of it, and kicked it over. There must have been a crater as well, just as there would be in France when a shell exploded. But I couldn't be sure whether I could identify that from here, the land was so uneven, hummocky, and strewn with debris.

Considering a busy mill had once thrived there, it was still a raw and ugly wound on the landscape.

Even in the last century, gunpowder wasn't made in a single structure but in stages. I knew only what I'd heard discussed by the officers in my father's command, debating the various kinds of gunpowder and their properties. I knew that it didn't "blow up" in the traditional sense of the word but expanded as it ignited. And I knew there was a rigid formula that produced the best powder, before being milled into small particles of equal size. Each stage was carried out in its own buildings, to lessen the danger of explosion. And so a powder mill was a collection of structures clustered among trees. Whatever had happened in this place had destroyed the lot. A single explosion powerful enough to create a chain reaction until there was nothing left.

Potassium nitrate—saltpeter—made a better gunpowder than sodium nitrate. And alder trees made the best charcoal for the formula. That was something else I'd heard. But for some time now gunpowder works all across Britain had begun to produce cordite instead of traditional black power, and that was a much more complicated recipe. With far more chances for something to go badly wrong. All I really knew was that the length and thickness of the "cord" in the manufacturing process determined how it would be used in munitions.

In 1915, a severe shortage of acetone, necessary to the process, had nearly shut down works all over the country. The loss of the Ashton Mill on the heels of that must have been devastating.

Though hardly an expert, I'd seen enough of the shelling in France to understand that here too something quite disastrous had happened, and that when it did, a great many people had died.

Pointing, Mark described the scene for me. "The walls were thicker on this side of the buildings, so that any blast would point away from the town just behind us. And the buildings were spaced for safety. Yet there's hardly a wall standing now. We'll never know how many survived the first blast. Or if any did." He paused, to let me resurrect the mill site in my mind. "When they took over the mill, the Government put in railway lines to bring in workers from The Swale villages. This was necessary to replace men who had enlisted. A good many of the new workers were women, along with some older workers from the brewery when it closed for lack of men. Three hundred souls to start with, and more as the demands of the war increased tenfold. Thank God it was a Sunday. The Fire Brigade came racing toward the blast, but there was no way to contain it or what followed. Several firemen were injured trying."

Turning slightly, he pointed north of where we were sitting. "That's The Swale." I could just see a line of blue water far to the right, at the foot of what appeared to be marshland. "It runs between the Medway to the west and the Thames Estuary to the east, and of course the Cran empties into it. Across

The Swale from us is the Isle of Sheppey. Quite marshy where it faces us, just as it is on this side. The abbots sent wool and barrels of mutton and hops and other goods down the Cran to ships waiting to cross to France. Much of the gunpowder went out the same way, to the munitions factories where the cartridges and various types of shells were filled. Artillery, Naval guns, mortars—whatever the War Office ordered. There used to be a small fishing fleet in Cranbourne as well, a survivor of the days of merchant ships."

I looked to my left. There was no sign of any railway station, nor the tracks coming into it. Both must have disappeared in the blast, save for a twisted length of iron that must have come from the train shed. I could pick that out now.

"We've never had any trouble. Not in over a *hundred years*. Not a single explosion."

I could hear the distress in his voice. The Ashtons had been proud of that record.

I remembered what he'd said earlier, that it was dangerous work, but paid well. And again that it was feared that the Government had been pushing too hard for larger and larger outputs of powder. After all, there was a war on . . .

The Cran was hardly more than a stream now, a narrow channel that must have been wider at one time. It would probably have been dammed long ago to feed the mill. A tidal river, presently at low tide, for the small craft anchored there were literally high and dry, tilted to one side, most of them waiting for the incoming flood to give them buoyancy once more.

I couldn't see what lay beyond the trees.

From something I'd heard the Colonel Sahib—my father—say, there were munitions factories somewhere out there on Sheppey, where women loaded shells and casings with the gunpowder brought from here. He would have known about them. And about the Ashton Powder Mill, surely. Of course there had never been any reason to speak of them to me. These were military matters.

I looked again at the ruins. Very much, I thought, like the abbey we'd passed, torn down by a very angry King. Only no one had wanted this rubble for Calais harbor. It lay where it had fallen two years earlier.

"Thank God, the tide was out that morning," Mark was saying. "A Sunday, no one about, no boaters or picnickers, no families strolling along the water. Only the men working inside. Or the toll could have been staggering. As it was, the blast took out windows for miles, lifted roofs right off the sheds on our side of the Cran, blowing in their doors. For that matter, we lost windows at Abbey Hall, and also part of the roof. Masts of ships in the Cran and The Swale were broken like sticks. And the earth shook like something demented. That was felt as far north as Norwich. Even Canterbury was badly shaken. There were any number of injuries all over this part of Kent, mostly from falling tiles and masonry or broken glass. Many people thought the Germans were shelling Canterbury."

I tried to imagine that morning, and failed. Frightened villagers rushing out of their houses to find out what had happened—and then, finally, *knowing*. And rushing on in horror to where we were sitting now. Their worst fears realized. A hundred men . . .

"The dust cloud was enormous. Stones rained down on everything. My mother heard them falling all around our house. I've always thought it was that dust cloud that set off the fire. Or at the very least fed it. But there's no way to prove that."

He sighed. "The main question after the explosion was, should the powder mill be rebuilt? The Government looked at the ruins, calculating the cost of removing all that rubble before they could begin. Asking themselves where to find the manpower to begin the task. But there was even a division of feeling about that. For some it was sacred ground, where their loved ones lay buried. For others it was well-paid work, and if the mill wasn't rebuilt, many would be unemployed. In the end, it was decided to expand a mill elsewhere. Although Captain Collier did everything in his power to convince the Army to rebuild, my father was blamed for their decision as well, accused of not fighting harder for reconstruction for the simple reason that the new powder works rising on the site would belong to the Government, not to him. And the mill has always been our greatest source of income. Not the sheep or the fields—the gunpowder. What's more, we couldn't begin to consider rebuilding ourselves. The cost would be prohibitive because of what had to be carried away even before we could start."

I had seen enough, and I was about to tell him so when an egg smashed into the windscreen directly in front of where I was sitting. Before I could stop myself, I threw up my hands to protect my face as it shattered. Another smashed on the bonnet, leaving a smear of yellow yolk.

Mark was swearing under his breath, already out of the motorcar, giving chase. It had happened so fast, I'd caught only a glimpse of whoever it was who'd thrown the eggs. A boy? A man? I could remember trousers—a cap pulled low. Mark, clearly, had seen him too, but I couldn't tell if he'd recognized the person.

I was also out of the car, shouting his name. He was too angry, and if he caught the miscreant, he was likely to do something he'd regret later.

Mark stopped just as he reached the shed corner. He'd forgot about me in that moment of blazing anger. And I realized, as I caught up with him and could look down the long line of sheds, that whoever it was had vanished— most likely into an open doorway— before Mark could follow him.

"Did you recognize him?" I asked.

"Worst luck, no." He stood there for a moment, then he turned back toward the motorcar. "It's hopeless. There are a hundred places he could hide."

"Has this happened before?" I asked, still shocked by the suddenness of the attack. "You mentioned property damage—this was very personal."

Shaking his head, he answered, "Nothing so direct, believe me." He helped me to climb into the motorcar again, and shut my door. "A wall or two pulled down. Sheep herded out into the marshes. A refusal by one of the shops in the village to fill my mother's order. The hop fields—they were once the abbey's—uprooted. The oast houses damaged. When we put up a watch, whoever it is seems to know where, and strikes at us in another part of the estate."

"And you said the local man refused to help. I expect he probably knew who might have done such things and didn't want to act."

Mark was quickly reversing, back to a point where he could turn the motorcar and return to the street that followed the abbey wall. "He called it high spirits. Restless lads, their fathers in France, their mothers out of work since the explosion. Constable Hood did come out, I'll give him that, looked around, shook his head, and said from the lack of evidence it was impossible to tell who might be responsible. It was true, of course, there was little to go by. But it was hardly helpful. And yes, my father also believed Hood had some idea who was behind what was happening, that was the worst part. And so the attacks went on. I think the constable must have known they would." His face was grim as he turned to me. "I'm sorry, Bess. I shouldn't have brought you down here to the river, but I thought—it seemed to be the best way to explain what happened."

"And this is why you wished to see the inspector in Canterbury."

"Nor was it the first time."

"But the explosion was what? Two years ago? It's under-
standable that people would have been upset at the time.
But now?"

"For over a year after any chance of sabotage had been dis-
counted, it was seen as a great tragedy. We were all affected
by what happened. My parents attended every one of the
memorial services. Then about four months ago—June, I
think it was, although I can't tell you precisely when, I was
in France—there was talk. At first a whisper, and before very
long a rumor. And then open speculation." He shook his
head. "Sometimes I have wished it *was* as simple as sabotage.
We'd be united in blaming the Germans."

"Yes," I responded slowly. "It's the whispers that are hard-
est to stop. And the rest follows."

He turned to me. "Shall I take you back to Canterbury?"

"Of course not. I'm made of sterner stuff than that." I
said it with a smile, and he returned it. But I could read the
embarrassment in his eyes.

"Good girl!" After a moment, he added, "They must have
thought you were Clara. Otherwise they wouldn't have
dared—" He broke off, still quite angry.

"Who is Clara?"

"My cousin. She's come to stay with us for a bit."

I wondered if the "bit" was since the troubles had started
or before.

It was even possible that with Mark only temporarily in
England, Mr. Ashton had arranged for Cousin Clara to be

there in the event that something happened to him. It was a foolish notion, I chided myself. Throwing eggs and tearing down walls in a field were not likely to escalate to murder. All the same, I couldn't quite shake off the feeling that things were beginning to change, and not for the better. And perhaps Philip Ashton had feared that from the start, setting his defenses quietly in place.

Chapter Two

WE WERE DRIVING down the lane that followed the abbey wall, branches of the trees marching beside us spreading like a canopy overhead. I could feel the tension lessening in both of us.

"Did Mother tell you? The Hall was once the old abbey guesthouse. It's been in the family for generations."

I could see it at the far end of the lane now, the same dark stone of the wall passing beside me, tall and quite old, with lovely windows framed in paler stone, some of them filled with diamond-paned glass. As we reached the door, the drive broadened into a circle. Over the door was a seal in an oval of richly colored stained glass.

"The abbot's coat of arms," Mark was saying, "although I have no idea which abbot. At a guess, it was the one who built the house."

The door flew open as if someone had been watching for us and a young woman—Clara?—with fair hair and an oval face came flying down the short flight of steps. As soon as she saw me, she stopped short, saying, "*Oh . . .*" as if a visitor was the last thing she expected.

Mark was out of the motorcar at once. "What is it?" he asked, as if fearful of bad news. "What's happened?"

"The morning post. More nasty unsigned letters threatening us. I tried to keep them from your mother, but I think she could read my face. She just held out her hand and I had no choice but to pass them over to her. Were you able to speak to Inspector—" She saw the slime of the egg on the bonnet. "Oh, dear. Where did this happen? Did you see who did it?" But her gaze turned to me, as if I'd been the cause of the egg throwing.

He hastily made the introductions as he opened my door to hand me out, then added, "Inspector Brothers wasn't in. Or so it was said. They wouldn't tell me when he'd be back. And so I came home. I brought Bess to cheer up Mother."

Clara said over her shoulder to me as she led the way inside, "Aunt Helen will be so pleased to see you." But there was little welcome in her tone of voice. "You're the Sister who took such good care of Mark? Yes, I thought so. I've heard Aunt Helen speak of you often."

We were in a large hall where what appeared to be a Georgian flight of stairs led to the upper floors. Passages led off to the right and left, embracing it. The exterior might be recognizable by the abbot who built the house, but sometime in the past, someone had taken it upon himself or herself to make the interior more fashionable. And dark woods had given way to brighter wallpapers. Here in the entrance it was a very handsome pale green printed with Chinese scenes, some of them picked out in gold leaf: the tips of the pagodas, the patterns on clothing, and the harnesses of horses catching the light.

"Where's Father?" Mark asked, setting my kit bag by the stairs as Clara and he turned to their right.

"In his study. Brooding, I think. I went in to ask him when he'd like his lunch, and he wasn't in the best of moods. At a guess, he'd decided he should have gone into Canterbury himself."

"That wouldn't have done at all. Take Bess in to see Mother. I'll go and speak to him."

He left me with Clara and went back the way we'd come, disappearing toward the far side of the stairs.

Clara opened the door into a sitting room decorated with blue-flowered wallpaper and a blue patterned carpet, giving it the air of a summer garden. I couldn't see Mrs. Ashton at first. Her chair was turned toward the windows as if to shut out the rest of the room. But when Clara said brightly, almost as one might to a child, offering a treat, "Aunt Helen? Mark has brought Sister Crawford to see you," she was out of her chair at once, staring at me.

"Is it you? Bess, dear, how wonderful to see you again." She came to me, embracing me, adding, "Where on earth did Mark find you?"

"I was in Canterbury this morning waiting for my train to London. I'm afraid it's been delayed. I went for a walk to pass the time, and Mark and I ran into each other by the cathedral."

"Yes, he's always liked Canterbury. But I thought he was going to"—she broke off, then quickly went on—"to run an errand for his father."

"Inspector Brothers wasn't in, and the desk sergeant wasn't very forthcoming about when he would return."

"Ah, you know about our situation. Just as well." She managed a smile. "There won't be any awkwardness now. Do come and sit down, Bess, and tell me how you are? Clara, could you ask Mrs. Byers to set another place for lunch, please?"

Clara said, "Of course," but left the room reluctantly, as if she'd prefer to share our chat.

Mrs. Ashton and I rearranged her pretty blue chair so that I could sit by her, and she asked my news. I tried to remember anything I'd heard recently about the Sisters and the doctors who'd worked on Mark's wounds, adding, "And I saw Matron not three weeks ago. They thought she'd caught the Spanish flu, but it was only a rather nasty cold."

"The Spanish flu has taken its toll here," she said. "Did Mark tell you about dear Ellie? Yes? Well, I must admit that it was an ordeal for all of us. And five of our neighbors didn't survive. Mark's old Nanny succumbed to it, as well as one of the housemaids. I'm glad Matron is all right. She's a remarkable woman. She was another one who refused to give up on

Mark." She glanced toward the door as we heard voices in the passage. "I've been happy to have Mark at home, even so briefly," she added quickly, lowering her voice, "although I know how eager he is to go back. Selfish of me, but he's my only child. I take each gift of time to heart."

The sitting room door opened and I looked up to see Mark and his father standing there. The resemblance between father and son was strong. At Mr. Ashton's heels was a liver-and-white spaniel. It stared at me with interest but was too well behaved to bark or come forward to sniff at my shoes.

The older man looked tired, and there were dark circles under his eyes, as if he hadn't slept well in some time. I thought too that he must be under a good deal of stress, for his coat was larger in the shoulders than it ought to have been, indicating he'd lost weight recently. Still, he smiled in genuine welcome and took my hand as Mark introduced us.

"I'm glad you've come," he said in a deep, warm voice. "If only to thank you for saving my son's life. But I must also apologize to you for the shocking behavior you witnessed there by the river. I wonder sometimes if the war hasn't brought out the worst in some people, just as it has the best in others."

"It was unexpected," I agreed, "but no harm done. I was grateful to Mark for showing me what a calamity had occurred here. I hadn't known." Mark had warned me not to speak of the explosion, but after Mr. Ashton had brought it up, I could hardly deny all knowledge of it.

"The Government thought it best not to publicize it." He went over and kissed his wife's cheek. I realized that he'd been out this morning as well, and she had been waiting anxiously for his return. It explained the chair turned toward the window, from which she could hear anyone coming up the drive.

"I've asked Bess to stay for lunch," she said to her husband.

"And I was about to suggest that she stay the night. From what Mark has said about these delays at the railway station, she won't see London before tomorrow morning late. Safer and more comfortable here, I should think."

I protested, not wishing to intrude, but Mr. Ashton frowned. "Nonsense. The hotels are crowded, and the railway people are likely to put off telling you that it's hopeless until it's too late to find a suitable room. There's nothing pressing in London, is there?"

Smiling, I thanked him and agreed. I had a little leave, I looked forward to seeing my parents, but a day more or less wouldn't matter. And truth be told, I wasn't particularly eager to find myself in a hotel the Nursing Service wouldn't approve of. It was very strict about such matters.

"Good, that's settled, then," he said, briskly rubbing his hands. He gestured to the spaniel and it went obediently to the hearth rug and settled for a nap. "Now to business. I saw to the mending of another stretch of stone wall—"

"Again?" Mrs. Ashton asked sharply. "You said nothing about it this morning."

"I didn't know then. Baxter came to fetch me as I was walking out. We attended to it ourselves. I've decided the less said, the better. No sense in encouraging others to try their hand at troublemaking."

Clara came then to tell us that lunch had been served. "A little early, but I thought you'd prefer it to tea. And Mrs. Lacey wants to look in on her sister this afternoon, if that's all right."

"Mrs. Lacey is our cook," Mrs. Ashton explained to me. "Her sister has been recovering from a chill and doesn't have her full strength back. Yes, do tell her to go on, my dear, and take a little of that soup her sister liked. It will keep up her strength."

She led the way to the dining room, along this same passage, and Mark followed with his father while Clara went to speak to Mrs. Lacey. The spaniel came with us and disappeared under the table.

It was a cold luncheon, and after eating whatever the hospital canteen could provide, I found it delicious. But Mrs. Ashton apologized for the shortages. "If we hadn't had the foresight to increase the number of hens we keep, we'd be no better than most. And much to our surprise, one of the housemaids is a marvel with them. As a girl, she looked after her mother's flock."

My mother had also looked to increase the chickens we kept in Somerset. Beef and pork allotments were stringently rationed, while chickens were a little less so if grown for a household.

It was a pleasant meal, and no one mentioned the problems facing the Ashtons and Abbey Hall. I was glad I had come here.

The Ashtons and Clara regaled me with descriptions of what it was like trying to communicate with poor Mark while he was as deaf as a post. Hasty searches for pen and paper when encountering him unexpectedly, falling back on shouting loudly in the hope of being understood, and then charades. They made it sound entertaining, but I knew it must have been very difficult for everyone. And Mark took it all with good grace, and laughed with us. But I could tell that his experience with silence had been worrying, because he'd never been able to believe his hearing would come back. I'd dealt with similar cases in France; I could read the signs.

We finished our meal and took our tea in Mrs. Ashton's sitting room. Even Clara seemed to be less ill at ease, realizing, I think, that I was only a temporary threat. I had to smile. Much as I cared for Mark, I wasn't in the market for a husband, certainly not with the war still going on. Then I found myself wondering how long she'd had this attachment to Mark. Since Eloise's death or before? Because attachment there was.

Then at two o'clock, without warning, everything changed.

AFTER THE TEA tray had been removed, Mark and his father went off to speak to someone about estate matters, and I could see that Mrs. Ashton was tiring. All that vivacious chatter at lunch had been a mask. It worried me, because I'd seen how strong she was in France when Mark's life lay in the balance. But she was under a great deal of stress, and I wondered if she was sleeping at all.

She offered to show me to my room, and on our way, Mrs. Ashton suggested that I might find the abbey grounds a pleasant place to stroll, if I cared for a little exercise after our lunch. "It's safe enough," she told me, "and Clara sometimes walks there." As I thanked her, I realized that this was the perfect excuse for me to allow Mrs. Ashton to rest, rather than entertain her unexpected guest. She gave me directions, urging me to treat this as my own home and enjoy myself, even offering to accompany me.

"You mustn't worry about me," I said, smiling. "If I can find my way across the north of France, I'll have no trouble. I only need to follow the abbey wall to a gate." And if further proof was necessary that I'd done the right thing, I noticed that she made no objection.

"Of course you can!" she'd answered brightly. "An hour? That should be just right to see everything."

I went down the drive with every intention of visiting the abbey ruins. Instead, when I reached the corner of the wall, I found myself walking back toward the river.

No one could mistake me for Clara now; my uniform would be the first thing anyone noticed. And so I felt relatively safe. Shocked as I'd been by the suddenness of the eggs flying at the motorcar, I had come to realize that they weren't intended for me, and indeed, neither egg had been meant to hit the passengers. It was just a show of meanness, and if I'd been the Ashtons, I'd have taken that to heart.

My own reason for going back was to get a better picture of the scene, because it had occurred to me at some point during lunch that once I reached London, I might ask my father, the Colonel Sahib, what he knew about the explosion and whether something could be done to ease the situation here before it actually became dangerous. If the police were taking such a hands-off attitude, perhaps the Army might have a quiet word in someone's ear about it. In India, my father had made something of a reputation for himself by defusing issues that way. The local people had come to respect him and understand that they could approach him. The remote hill tribes were a mutual enemy, and that had helped smooth the way too—no one wanted to find *them* on the doorstep, taking advantage of our troubles.

As it was, I found the quay deserted. The tide was only just turning, hardly stirring the beached boats. A pair of seagulls, spotting me, came flying out of nowhere to inspect me in case I was bringing their luncheon. They were raucous, and intent on making sure I knew they were about, but I ignored them.

This close I could get a better view of the ruins. I could see where Mr. Ashton must have forded the river before realizing that there was nothing to be done for those caught in the blast. I paused, looking to my right toward The Swale, and the low-lying

Isle of Sheppey beyond. Marshy indeed, there, and also on the far side of the Cran below the mill. There the land sloped, running down to The Swale, while on this side of the Cran, rising ground kept the land dry, fit for sheep and hops and whatever else the abbey and now the Ashtons chose to grow.

I was shading my eyes with my hand for a better look at the island, cut off from the Kent mainland by The Swale, when someone spoke from just behind me, making me jump.

"The Isle of Sheep. It's what *Sheppey* means."

I turned. Several of the shed doors had stood open as I walked along the river, but the interiors had appeared to be empty. Now, in the one nearest me, a man was lighting a cigarette. Then he leaned back against the frame.

He must, I thought, have heard the gulls and stepped out to see what they were on about.

Tall, but not as tall as Mark, fair, hazel eyes, his expression lively with curiosity.

"Sorry. I didn't mean to startle you. I was working behind the boat."

I could see a rather large sailboat hull sitting on a cradle in the dimness of the interior behind him. His hands were covered in dust, as if he'd been sanding, and I could see flecks of it on his face. I couldn't help but wonder if he'd been the egg thrower. Or knew who it was.

Without waiting for an answer, he went on. "You're a nursing Sister. Did you bring someone to Cranbourne? Anyone I might know?"

"Actually, I'm a guest at Abbey Hall," I said.

He frowned. "Indeed."

"I was one of Major Ashton's nurses. I met his mother when she came over to find him."

"Ah. And so you've walked down to see the scene of the tragedy."

Turning back to the river, I said, "It's not the best of times to be a visitor. Earlier someone threw eggs at the motorcar when Major Ashton brought me here."

"Not a very friendly welcome," he agreed. "If you're wondering if I threw them, the answer is no." But from the tone of his voice I gathered he'd have preferred something a little more lethal.

"As a matter of interest, were you here when the mill exploded?"

"I was." He looked with distaste at the cigarette he was holding, then pitched it in the river beyond us.

"Not working in here, surely?" I asked, gesturing toward the open shed.

"God, no. The doors were blown in, and the place was a disaster. Paint and varnish and all the rest scattered every which way." He inclined his head in the direction of the hull. "I hadn't begun this one—or it would probably have been matchwood."

"You're a boat builder?"

"I was, until the war put an end to it. No one is buying pleasure craft these days."

"I expect not."

"There was a flying club out on Sheppey. I was a member, as it happened. When war came, I wanted to fly. Early in 1916 I crashed coming in with a machine that was barely holding itself together. That put paid to my war. I should have gone down at sea." He pointed to his foot. "A softer landing, if a wet one."

I could see that his right boot was high, protecting a stiff ankle.

"Not much use when you can't fly any longer. Even the Army wouldn't take me. Hardly surprising, if you can't climb the ladder when the whistle blows," he went on. "Or race across No Man's Land. There's a splinter of something nasty lodged near my heart as well. No one would operate. And there you have it."

I thought perhaps he'd explained his presence out of a sense of guilt for not being in France. There were uniforms for the wounded who couldn't be returned to duty. He was wearing worn corduroy trousers and a cotton shirt to work in. "It's very dangerous to try," I said. "But you can still build your boats. There's something to be said for that." Then I realized how neatly he'd changed the subject so that he hadn't had to talk about the explosion.

"This is a perfect place for such a mill," I went on. "I don't see why they decided not to rebuild on this same site." Two could play at this game of misdirection.

"It would cost more and take longer to clear the land before putting up another building. They've moved on. Besides, it's a grave now, isn't it?" He pointed to the line of warehouses. "It was rumored they might turn these into a new factory. But the town protested, and I think it finally dawned on London that where there had been one catastrophe, there could very well be another, and this time, the town—or a large part of it, at any rate—might go up with the buildings. They were damn—very lucky, the last time."

"But why was it suspicious, this blast?"

He answered grudgingly, "Ashton Powder had had a very good record. The mill had been here since the Napoleonic Wars, if not before, and there had never been any trouble. That's rare, dealing with gunpowder."

"Then what went wrong two years ago?" I persisted.

"People got careless. Or nervous. One mistake is all it takes to level such a place. And there was the pressure to produce more and more powder. The munitions factories were running flat out. Collier did his best to keep them busy. God, if you were in France, you've heard the guns, you know how many they lob over in a single hour. All those shells have got to come from somewhere. And the powder to fill them."

I knew, all too well. The ground shook, the very air seemed to vibrate as the big guns pounded a sector. Men lost their hearing, as Mark had done, or had such severe headaches they couldn't function. Some developed such a shock to the nervous system that they couldn't stand.

All those shells have got to come from somewhere . . .

I turned back to the ruins. "You don't think about that, do you? Where the shells come from. It just seems there's an endless supply." Changing the subject, I said, "Does *everyone* in Cranbourne believe that Mr. Ashton started that fire?"

"There are two camps. The survivors of those lost in the explosion needed someone to blame. A casual spark seems a very dubious source for such tragedy. After all, as I said, it had never happened before. And Ashton was there. As it began."

"And the other camp?"

"They've lost their livelihood, haven't they? And they too want to blame someone."

"Are you among those last?"

He shrugged. "I'd like to hold someone responsible too. I knew many of the men who were killed. It's comforting, you know, to find someone to blame. It says that God isn't cruel, it's Man who caused such pain and loss. You can rage at a man. It's harder to rage at God."

He hadn't really answered my question, but I let it go. I was starting to walk on, when he said, "Let me close these doors. I'll walk back with you."

I could see his limp as he shut the long, heavy doors. He didn't bother to lock them. Coming to join me where I stood watching the tide run in fast, he said, "They wouldn't put a hospital here, you know. Even though the Ashtons and others with large houses offered. Too close to the mill."

"That's interesting," I said. We walked a little way, and I asked, "How *did* the fire start? The explosion was bad enough."

"Nobody knows. But it put paid to any attempt to find out how the explosion occurred. Or to look for survivors who might have known the truth."

Which must have pointed an even stronger finger at Philip Ashton.

The man was looking closely at me. "You're very curious about all this."

"Wouldn't you be?" I gestured toward the blackened ruins. "Even two years after the explosion, it's frightful. So many lives lost?" I shook my head. "If there is any place where ghosts walk, it's there, across the river."

I'd meant it metaphorically, not literally. But I saw the shock in his eyes before he turned away.

"Do you believe in ghosts?" he asked after a moment as we left the river behind and turned toward the abbey.

"I don't know," I replied. "I've never seen one."

He didn't quite know how to take that answer.

We parted company at Abbey Lane, and he nodded to me before turning to go. "Enjoy your stay," he said. With bare politeness.

"Thank you," I said. And as I walked back to Abbey Hall, I wondered what he'd seen in those ruins that had made him take me so literally when I spoke of ghosts.

WHEN I WALKED into the hall, Clara was just coming down the stairs. "There you are! Aunt Helen is lying down. Is there anything I can do for you? Do you remember the way to your room?"

"Yes, I do, thank you, Clara." Turn right at the top of the stairs. Third door on my right. "I'm sorry to put everyone to such trouble."

"It's no trouble at all. Would you like to see Aunt Helen's garden?

It's a part of the old abbey, and quite lovely. I shouldn't wonder if it had been an herb garden. Monks knew a great deal about healing. Somehow it has managed to survive for centuries. That's rather remarkable."

"I remember your aunt talking about it to Mark while he was feverish," I said lightly. "I'll enjoy seeing it."

We walked in silence to a door at the side of the house that opened into the garden. And we stepped out into a little bit of paradise.

There were still herbs, many of which I recognized, in beds that were separated by perennials. And in the stone wall itself here and there were pockets of tiny wildflowers that spilled down in miniature falls of color. As if holding on to summer as long as possible in this protected space. At the bottom of the garden was a slightly raised terrace where graceful iron chairs, painted white, sat beneath an arbor that was thick with wisteria vines, still green. That, I thought, must be Helen Ashton's personal contribution to this wonderful space.

"This is really lovely." But as we stepped out into it, I began to notice that no one had deadheaded the blooming plants or trimmed the wisteria recently, a measure of how little time Mrs. Ashton had spent here of late. A measure too of her worry?

Stopping to admire a display of flowers I didn't recognize, I became aware of Clara's frown.

"You nursed Mark when he was so ill? Aunt Helen came home singing your praises. She said you saved his life with your care and your training."

She was jealous. I'd realized that but hadn't expected her to be so blunt about it.

I smiled. "That's very kind of her," I said quietly. "The truth is we had the best doctors imaginable and an experienced nursing staff. And Mark wasn't the only miracle they've worked."

"Yes, well, Aunt Helen seldom mentions them."

I said, turning to look straight at her, "I've nursed hundreds of men since I finished my training. Mark was special because his mother had come to help us in any way she could, and we didn't want to let her down. We didn't want to have to tell her one morning that her son hadn't lived through the night."

She stared at me as if I'd bitten her.

"I see" was all she could manage before she turned away. Then, without looking at me, she added, "I'm so sorry. It's just that she's so very happy to have you here. And Mark is as well."

"I expect my arrival helped to take their minds off what's been happening. What's the old expression? A change of trouble is as good as a holiday? Sometimes it's true."

To my surprise, she flushed, saying again, "I'm so sorry. I— Mark and I—I've been in love with him since I was fourteen."

"Then you've nothing to fear from me."

"Thank you," she said ruefully. But we both knew that Eloise was her rival still. And that was as it should be. Mark would have to mourn before he could turn elsewhere.

We walked on, down to the terrace, where I admired the small pools that had been put in on either side.

"The monks would have kept fish in the pools," she said. "Stocked for use as needed on holy days. Alas, there are none in here now. There was a story I read once, when I was a child. About a monk who had made friends with the carp in the fishpond, only to discover that a curse had been put on it, and when the curse was lifted, a prince stepped out of the water. In gratitude, the prince built a great abbey where only a poor wooden one had stood. I remember coming here as a little girl, looking for the fish, determined to find the prince."

We laughed together as we turned back toward the house. But her prince had found another princess. Eloise had got there first.

Over the wall, toward the front of the house, came the sounds of carriages coming up the drive. Their pace didn't sound like that of casual visitors. Too brisk, the wheels rattling loudly. I could hear one OF THE DRIVERS reining in the horses.

Clara's face was white. "Oh, God, who can that be?"

Side by side we hurried up the garden to the door into the house. I could hear someone coming down the stairs. Mrs.

Ashton. She called to her housekeeper, and there was fear in her voice.

We reached the hall just as a fist pounded on the door.

Clara started forward. Mrs. Ashton barred her way. "Let Mrs. Byers open the door. Come with me to the study."

Mark was already standing there on its threshold, listening, his gaze going to his mother's face as the three of us hurried toward him. Behind him, Mr. Ashton had risen from his desk.

I watched as the housekeeper came up from the kitchen, walking steadily toward the sound of the knocking, but before Mark could shut the study door behind us I saw that Mrs. Byers's hands were clenched in the fabric of her dress.

Mr. Ashton was at the window now. He said to his wife, "It's nothing to worry about, my dear. I expect it's the police. They've found our young vandals."

"They'll want us to be magnanimous and not press charges," Mark answered him, but there was bitterness in his voice.

As if by agreement, we took chairs, trying to look as if this was no more than a social call. Mark replaced his father by the windows, his back to the room, while his father resumed his seat behind the desk. As voices reached us from the hall, I heard a low growl and realized that the spaniel was under the desk at its master's feet. Mr. Ashton spoke to it, and it was quiet again.

After what seemed an eternity, we heard Mrs. Byers's tentative tap on the door, and then it swung open.

All of us, except for Mark, could see the man standing there, and the uniformed policemen behind him. He was of medium height, perhaps forty-five, dark haired. There was a grim expression on his face.

Not one of us believed now that this call was about young vandals.

My heart flew into my throat, and I reached out for Mrs. Ashton's hand. She clasped my fingers fiercely until they hurt.

Philip Ashton rose. "Inspector Brothers," he said calmly.

"Good afternoon, Mr. Ashton. I've come from Canterbury with a warrant for your arrest for the murder of these men." He held out several sheets of paper, and I could see that they were filled with names. "I shall be happy to read them to you, sir, if you insist."

"I know the names of these dead," Mr. Ashton said. "They are engraved on my soul. What evidence is there that I have caused their deaths?"

"You were at the mill earlier in the day, Sunday the second of April 1916, before the first blast, behaving suspiciously, and there again just after the explosions brought the buildings down, standing at the very spot where the flames rose as you were hurrying away. This has been attested to by a dozen people who have come forward and given their depositions. They were rushing toward the river, and they report that your expression as you turned their way was gleeful."

"Gleeful? I see. And what possible motive could I have had for destroying my mill, much less wanting these men dead?"

"A court will hear that in due course, sir. I am here to take you into custody on the charges brought."

"Yes, certainly." He glanced toward his wife, standing still as if turned to stone, her blue eyes stark in her pale face. "Will you give me a few minutes to say good-bye to my family, and to give my son instructions about my affairs?" I could see Inspector Brothers hesitate. "I give you my word, Inspector. I will come through that door in ten minutes' time and accompany you to Canterbury without fuss."

Reluctantly—I think he was all too aware of the constables at his back, prepared for any resistance—the Inspector agreed. Stepping back into the passage, he shut the door, and all of us could hear his voice issuing abrupt orders for his men to wait outside.

I would have left, to give them privacy, but Mrs. Ashton was still gripping my hand as if it were a lifeline to hope.

Philip Ashton came across the room to her and put his arm around her shoulders, pulling her close. "Nothing to worry about, my dear, it will all be resolved shortly. I want you to be brave and not do anything rash."

I couldn't imagine Mrs. Ashton doing anything rash, but I thought the words were meant for Mark as well.

He nodded to me, then turned to his niece. Clara was striving to hold back tears as she said good-bye.

"It might be best for you to go home," he urged her. "Will you think about it?"

And then he was conferring in a low voice with his son, close by the window.

Without looking at us, three women still standing there like marble statues, unable to speak, he crossed the room. Mrs. Ashton put out her hand then as if to stop him, but let it drop. He opened the door, stepped through it, then shut it firmly behind him, and we could just hear voices as Inspector Brothers took him in charge. As well as the soft *clink* of handcuffs.

The spaniel went to the door, scratching on it and whining.

About the Author

CHARLES TODD IS the author of the Inspector Ian Rutledge mysteries, the Bess Crawford mysteries, and two stand-alone novels. A mother and son writing team, they live in Delaware and North Carolina.

Discover great authors, exclusive offers, and more at hc.com.